If
Loving Me
Is
Wrong

JJV: The Storyteller

If Loving Me Is Wrong

ACKNOWLEDGMENTS

In every other acknowledgement during this series, I saved thanking God for last. He was always last, but not least. Well in this acknowledgment, I want to thank Him first. I do all things through Christ who strengthens me. I want to acknowledge you, Lord, for all your blessings that you have bestowed upon me and continue to bestow on me. Thank You, Almighty Father.

My support system is strong and has primarily been the same people that have been there since the release of *Can't Nobody*. I really appreciate your continued support, love and encouragement given to me throughout this journey. I stepped out on faith, leaving a lucrative job to follow what God has guided me to do. As a result, I do hope that you have found this series entertaining, but also inspirational. Throughout my writings, I have embedded things that God has placed in my heart.

I know that January 20, 2017, seemed like a bleak day for some of us in America. But I see it as one of the greatest opportunity for God to lead our country through what needs to be done. It is time for us to put God first, and allow Him to lead our journey. One man or woman will not change our destiny. I am praying not only for America, but for the world to receive the revelation knowledge it needs to be able to complete this earthly journey.

In closing, I think it is imperative that we recognize that we all are from one race, the human race. One love to all and thank you for your support!

DEDICATION

"Time can never diminish the power of REAL love." jjv

INTRODUCTION

Although I attended four years of seminary school and graduated at the top of my class, it took me a while to truly grasp the concept of self-love. Some would say that self-love is boastful, prideful, and conceited. Many shone away from doing things for themselves and or for the benefit of one's self, because they don't want to appear selfish. However, I challenge those who don't understand the real concept of love to stretch the boundaries of one's own self-limiting behaviors and embrace the real meaning of self-love.

It is understood by all believers that the greatest commandment that God gave us was to love Him with all of our heart and mind. Many Christians know that the second greatest commandment is to love your neighbor as you love yourself. It took critical self-analysis for me to understand that within the second greatest commandment, God had given me the permission to love myself. I tell everyone I meet these days, using the words of a wise friend who once told me that, "If loving me is wrong, I don't want to be right."

Chapter 1

On my first day of seminary school, I was not certain I had made the right decision. I was comfortable with my facts and everything having a place that could be verified within my qualitative world. I was not prepared for an environment where people talked about things like creation and the nature of the relationship between God and people.

Although I was baptized, and believed in Jesus, I did not necessarily theorize on such subjects. I was more concerned about how God could help me survive in the context within the world I lived. I faced a lot of pain in my life, and before I had met the Light, I did not even believe there was a God. I knew that no God would allow certain things to happen to good people. However, when I met the Light, He told me to trust in Him, and He would guide me.

I put all of my trust in Him and He got me through the death of Aunt Hattie, the one person that I loved and trusted the most in this world. He also helped me accept many things that I could not change. Things like, finding out that my dad was a sexual molesting monster who abused his own daughter; growing up hating my cousin,

Mystery, who turned out to be my mother; discovering Ty, the only man that I ever trusted and loved, enjoyed having sex with men; and losing a baby when I did not even know I was pregnant.

I look back on those days and don't know how I could have made it without Him. This was my experience with God and believing in Him. My primary purpose in attending seminary school was to learn more about Him, so I could help other people gain a deeper understanding of who He is, and lead nonbelievers to believe in Him.

By the time I entered Duke Divinity School, I was in a good place. I had forgiven Ty, and could carry on a long distance, platonic friendship with him. I loved my mother and had a fairly decent relationship with her, as compared to my younger days when I cursed at her daily just for breathing. I gained two additional family members, my mother's sister, Auntie Char, and my mother's husband, Sweezy. I also developed a close personal relationship with Sadiq, the pastor of my church.

Most people would have said that Sadiq and I were dating, but it was a little different from the relationship I had shared with Ty. Ty was the first and only man I ever had sex with; while Sadiq was a man of the cloak, who took his position very seriously. We did not engage in any intimate physical contact, except for an occasional kiss. For months, I told everyone that we were friends, until he confirmed that we were dating, without the benefit of sex.

IF LOVING ME IS WRONG

During my first year at Duke Divinity School, Mystery spent a lot of time with me. My extra room, which I had initially set up as my study room, ended up being her bedroom. There were many weekends I had three additional people in my 700 square foot space, Sadiq, who always slept on the sofa, and Mystery and Sweezy who slept in the extra room. We would literally be on top of each other when the four of us were in my apartment.

Mystery and I had only one big argument during my first year at seminary school. Luckily, the guys were not around, because it got nasty. Mystery ended up catching a plane back to Houston, only to return three days later with a box Jacques Torres chocolates. Since I no longer was an athlete, I found myself indulging in things like fine chocolates, and Mystery knew that I could not resist the finest of all chocolates. I could not tell you today, what the fight was about, but Mystery and her chocolates were definitely welcomed in my home.

Initially, I had a difficult time accepting Mystery and Sweezy's relationship, because Sweezy was my deceased best friend's boyfriend. I eventually became comfortable with their relationship after I saw that Mystery loved Sweezy as much as he loved her. I realized I had no right to hold Sweezy accountable to a dead person. Mystery and Sweezy spent a lot of time with me because they were opening a business venture in Charlotte. I knew they could afford a hotel in Charlotte, but I think it was Mystery's way of making certain she watched over me.

Sweezy and I had a close relationship when he dated my deceased best friend, Chanti, but we developed an even closer relationship when he married Mystery. Although Sweezy was not much older than me, I viewed him as a father figure. I knew I could trust him with any and everything. He often ran interference between Mystery and I, serving as the peacemaker. I could confide in him with just about everything, and often asked for his male perspective when I faced issues that I did not understand.

I wanted to have as close of a relationship with Mystery as I did with Sweezy, but it was difficult because Mystery would go into a protective mother mode and try to fix everything for me. I once told Mystery about one of my professors, whom I thought might be racist, and she called the school to speak with the professor. I had to drop his class and replace it with another one. I knew Mystery's intentions were good, but she did not always react in a rational manner. I spent a lot of time trying to change Mystery, but experience taught me that I would have to love Mystery just the way she was.

My best time away from North Carolina was spending time at Aunt Hattie's with Auntie Char, whose real name was Chardonnay. She was so opposite of Mystery. Auntie Char was two years older than Mystery but had experienced a lot of trauma during her lifetime. She was humble and comforting. She reminded me a lot of Aunt Hattie. Anytime I had a problem, I felt comfortable enough to speak with Auntie Char.

The two of us would go on outings and have a blast when I visited. Mystery, at times, openly stated how she did not like me spending so much time with Chardonnay. According to Mystery, she did not completely trust Chardonnay's intentions. Although Mystery loved Chardonnay, she had good reasons for not trusting her completely. I never asked Mystery for her reasons, because I wanted Aunt Char and my relationship based on my experiences with her. I also knew that Mystery had a difficult time letting go of the past. She did not mind letting people know that she could forgive, but she was not one easy to forget.

Of all the relationships I had during my first year of school, by far, the strangest was with Ty. I could not explain it, but with everything we went through, I still loved him. He begged me over and over again to give him another chance, but I could not. The trust was not there.

During my first year, Ty married some older woman who died within a few days of them being married. Ty also became the legal guardian of his little sister, Penny, who I became very fond of. I kept in close contact with her on a weekly basis. I really liked her a lot, but, if I were to be completely honest, I think it was also a way for me to keep dibs on Ty.

These people were all part of my support system the first year. I would not have made it without my home crew. My professors all seemed distant, but my academic advisor, Chrissy Richards, was definitely God-sent. I found myself in a space of self-doubt many times throughout the year. Chrissy would listen more than she talked. Every now and then, she would make suggestions, but for the most part, it was good having her around to listen to me because there were way too many days I had my bags packed, ready to return to Houston.

Chapter 2

I had somewhat of a difficult time adjusting to life at Duke. The first thing that hit me like a brick in the face was the number of blacks that were not present at the school. There was a teaspoonful of us, and none of them seemed to be on the journey that I was on. I attempted to speak to several of them, but they always started rambling in terms I had never heard. I don't mean words, but speaking esoterically, all I could do was cut the conversation short and run. I was so accustomed to being around black folks that I considered real. Yeah, I had my issues with them too, but at least I understood where they were coming from.

I became uncertain about my destiny and what I thought was my purpose. These folks did not look like me, did not speak like me, nor did they act like me. Not to mention, most of them came from different backgrounds. I grew up in Third Ward, which was an inner-city community within Houston. Most of the students I encountered were white males from suburban or rural areas in the mid-west and the east coast. There were not a lot of students from the south. Our culture and lifestyles were worlds apart.

Even the folks I met that were from North Carolina were different. I always thought folks in North Cackalacky were southern folks, but I could not even find a good fried turkey leg, much less some gumbo that did not taste like it came out of a can. This was the first time I realized that there was a real Cajun influence on those of us who lived in Houston. I began to truly understand that Houston was really an extension of Louisiana, because of the large migrant population from Louisiana to Texas, and that southern did not mean Cajun or Creole.

What affected me the most was that I was no longer the smartest person in the class. Many of the students had been on their journey for a while. I was new to all of this, as I had just met the Light a few months prior. They were already dedicated to a life of Christian-living, and knew more than anything that this was their predestined journey.

I was trying to learn more about God and Christianity. I was coming from a state of ignorance and discomfort with my own understanding of myself, who I was, how I fit into the world, and knowing my mission. I could spit out an answer in my sleep if asked, what is the difference between centripetal acceleration and centrifugal force? However, now I was being asked, *is it possible for predestination and free will to co-exist biblically?* I had no idea what that meant, much less any notion about how to answer. I felt completely out of my element.

I took a course on atheism and found myself on trial throughout the course. I begged Chrissy to let me out of this class, but she insisted I stayed and told me that I would eventually excel in this class. In the end, she was correct. This class helped me explain concepts around Christianity with more clarity than I had ever spoken. It boosted my confidence in my ability to make it through the first year. However, I innately knew that my trust in God, support from my family, and the ear of Chrissy, would help me during this phase in my life. But of all the relationship I had and/or recently established, the relationship I developed with Mookie Davis ended up carrying me through.

I was near the end of my second semester of school when I was walking from one of my classes and heard a male voice say, "Hey, wait up." I looked back thinking that perhaps it was someone from the Ward.

I once ran into a girl at the mall who said, "Hi Porchia. What are you doing here?" I looked at her and asked her how she knew my name. She happened to be a girl that was in my chemistry class, that I knew well, but because she was in North Carolina, I did not recognize her.

I was hesitant to say that I did not know this guy, so I waited until he came closer. There was no way I had ever met this guy. He was a little taller than me, with a medium brown complexion, wore shoulder-length dreads, had dark blue-green eyes with long eyelashes, thick dark eyebrows, dimples, beautiful straight white teeth, and a goatee.

I must have given him a weird look because he quickly said, "I have seen you around and just wanted to introduce myself to you. I am Mookie Davis." He reached out his hand for me to shake it. I found myself just staring at him because I had never seen someone with such a striking and beautiful face, especially his eyes. He then said, "My hand is getting tired, Ms. Lady. Are you going to shake it or what?"

"My bad, my name is Porchia," I replied as I reached out and shook his hand.

"Wow, Ms. Lady, you have a serious grip!"

I laughed and eased up on the shake. "I didn't hurt you, did I?"

"Nah, I've felt worse. Porchia, huh? I like that name."

"Thanks, my mom thought she was naming me after a car, but she really did not know how to correctly spell Porsche."

"Real?"

"Yep, really." I said smiling.

"That's what's up. What set do you claim?" "Huh?" I asked.

"Where are you from?"

"Houston."

"Oh, H-Town. I used to run there." "Oh, you were a track star?" I asked.

Mookie laughed and said, "Nah, Ms. Lady, but you are cute."

"And you have beautiful eyes," I said. "Yeah, they got me caught up a lot." "Caught up?" I asked.

"Yeah, well, I would like to know more about the lady named after a car. Can I get your number?"

"Let me get yours." I said.

"Like that huh? Okay." Mookie recited his number and I saved it in my phone. "Well, Ms. Lady, I hope you use it."

I smiled. "It was nice meeting you, Mookie. Is that the name your Mom gave you?"

"Yeah, Ms. Lady, that is my government name."

I laughed. "I am not certain what government would name someone Mookie, but okay."

"Nah, but my street name is Gig."

"Gig? I think I prefer Mookie."

"You can call me anything you want, as long as you call me."

I laughed and said, "I am running late. Will be in contact soon."

"I'll hold you to that."

I walked away smiling because Mookie was actually refreshing. Most of the people I encountered were either too stuffy or too serious. I was not certain what was up with Mookie, but I knew that he would at least be entertaining. After all, with a nickname like Gig, he had to be.

I decided to go home before my next class, and when I arrived, I saw that I had company. Mystery and Sweezy were sitting locked in a passionate kiss on my sofa.

"Oh, yuck. Go get a hotel room!" I said.

Sweezy jumped up and said, "Why are you not in school, Swoosh?"

"Oh, so this is what my sex-crazed parents do when I am out learning more about my Savior?"

"Hi, Porchia, I am sorry that I did not call to let you know that we were coming. I wanted to surprise you, and figured that you would not mind," Mystery said, while standing and trying to straighten out her clothes.

"I don't know about her, but I came cuz I missed you, Swoosh!" Sweezy ran over to me and began squeezing me.

I pulled away and said, "It is not me that it looks like you are missing. What is up with you two?"

Mystery looked at me and said, "I will make a pot of coffee. We have some news for you."

"Mystery, I ain't got time for coffee. I have another class in an hour. What's up?" I asked.

She grabbed my hand and led me to the sofa and pretty much pushed me down and said, "Have a seat."

"Mystery, you are scaring me. What's up?"

"Queen! Stop making a mini-series out of it. Swoosh, you're having a li'l bro," said Sweezy.

Mystery chimed in, "Sweezy, we don't know the sex yet."

I jumped up, hugged Mystery and said, "Congratulations on whatever you are having. I am excited for you."

I remembered how hard it was on Mystery when she lost her first baby, so I quickly prayed that she would be able to bring this one to term. It was as if Mystery needed to be a mother, since she did not have the real chance to raise me. I looked at Sweezy and he was standing there like a proud papa.

"Congrats to you too, Pappa Sweezy," I said laughing.

"Funny you should call me Pappa Sweezy because I told Queen that we would have to name the boy Pappasumthin, as much as she been feening food from Pappadeaux's and Pappa's Seafood!"

I laughed; then asked, "So, how far along are you, Mystery?"

"I am in my second trimester."

"Where are you hiding the baby?" I asked.

Mystery patted her butt and said, "I know you see all this bootay on me, girl."

"Nah, Queen, that was there before," Sweezy said with a smirk on his face.

"If you eva wanna get some more of this bootay, you betta keep quiet, Sweezy," Mystery said while laughing.

"Okay, you two, I hate to break up this lovefest, but I have to get back to my classes. We'll have to celebrate when I get out of school."

"Okay, we need to go check on the club. So let's plan on dinner for eight tonight," said Mystery.

"Sounds like a plan to me," I kissed Mystery on her cheek and went into my room to grab my tablet, which I had forgotten earlier.

Mystery shouted from the living room that they were leaving. I told them to drive carefully and I would see them later tonight.

I felt some relief knowing that they were leaving. I was truly happy for them, but I was not certain how I felt about having a little brother or sister. I was barely comfortable with the idea that Mystery was my mother, much less a little sibling entering the picture.

I had half brothers and sisters, from my child molesting father that I visited from time-to-time, but I did not get to spend quality time with them. Of course, my sister, Tracy, and I were tight, but she and I were always best of friends. This situation made me think about Ty and Penny. Although she was a sweet child, and I had developed a close relationship with her, still I had to wonder, *could I actually be a good big sister?*

I sighed knowing that I had another request to add to my exhaustive prayer list. I sometimes thought that God determined that I had too many prayers to answer, so He would decide on which ones were most important.

Chapter 3

I ran into Mookie about two weeks later, after a rally against the Supreme Court for ruling that prayer in public school was illegal. He walked up to me with a serious look on his face and said, "Hey, Ms. Lady, I am so glad to see you. I was rushed to the hospital because I stopped breathing and almost died."

"Oh no, I am sorry to hear that. What happened?"

"Well, they found me sitting with my phone in my hand, holding my breath, waiting for you to call."

The old Porchia would have told him to fuck off, that he was full of shit, but the new Porchia smiled. "I have been crazy busy. But what are you getting into now? Would you like to go grab something to eat?"

He agreed to join me. Mookie was definitely an interesting character. Mookie's father was a lieutenant for the LAPD, and his mother was a principal at a high school located in Compton, California where they lived. He said his parents insisted on living in the community in which they served. Mookie told me that he had an older sister who was a doctor at MLK Community Hospital, and a younger brother who was an Assistant District Attorney for the County of Los Angeles.

15

The next part of Mookie's life took me through a whirlwind. Mookie was a notorious member of one of the most highly publicized and notorious gangs within the Los Angeles area. He had been shot five times, arrested dozens of times, and had committed acts that he said he could never speak about to anyone. However, Mookie's connections kept him above the law.

Mookie also confessed, because of his connections, he had to do heinous acts to prove that he was down for his crew. Mookie showed me his battle scars, and told me they served as a reminder of what God delivered him from. He said his life was destined to end with death, by either the streets, prison, or his former gang members; however, only by the grace of God, did he escape.

After Mookie finished his story, I did not know whether to run or celebrate. When he spoke about his past, he had a total different look than the guy I first saw trying to holla at me. Sweezy and Big John were the closest people I knew that formerly lived a life of crime.

Something told me that Mookie's journey was very different from theirs. Sweezy and Big John sought out crime as a means to economic freedom; whereas, it seemed that Mookie was attempting to escape from something. He had good role models, but chose a life of crime. For me, two plus two equaled some other number than four.

I told Mookie that everyone probably has a story to tell, but his story was exceptional, and could only serve as motivation to others. I think I saw a tear form in

Mookie's eye as he changed the subject from his past back to talking about school. He wanted to know how I was getting along in the racially, sexually, socially and economically non-diverse school.

After I confided in him that it was a battle for me, he told me that he was thinking about approaching the administration to see if he could assist with recruiting minorities, females, and economically and socially disadvantaged students for admission.

I understood Mookie's cause, but I wondered whether there were students that wanted to go to the school and not allowed admission. My story was a little different. I was not only allowed admission, but was accepted late and given a full scholarship. I did not have any complaints about the way I was treated by the school.

It was just uncomfortable for me to be around so many homogeneous people who all seemed to dress, act, and think alike. I became uncomfortable speaking up in class, so most of the time I just listened to them. After all, it was a learning experience for me since they had life experiences, that seemed not only unreal, but also unimaginable to me.

Our relationship flourished from that day forth. Mookie took his spiritual life serious, but still had a rough edge about him that he would only show when we were alone. We tackled the cause for diversifying the school with much opposition from the administration. They insisted that the school afforded equal opportunity to anyone who applied. We argued that if that was true, the school did not perform proper outreach to the communities in need, to assist them financially and encourage or engage communities for the inclusiveness needed to have a diverse student body.

We prepared position papers with the help of an affirmative action organization that made a case to the University that they may not be intentionally discriminating, but the numbers for female and minority students were not reflective of the community or similar seminary schools across the country.

Mookie would sometimes amuse me with the manner in which he presented information to the executive staff. Whenever he felt that he was being unfairly challenged or denigrated in any fashion, he would go South Central on them.

Once a professor, that was known to have very conservative views, questioned the statistics that reflected the number of African Americans that should be present in North Carolina seminary schools. Mookie looked directly at him and asked, "Can you count the number of African American students you have had in your class over the last four years?"

The professor stuck out his chest and started naming students, which amounted to about six students. Mookie then asked the professor if he could name the white male students that he had over the last four years. The professor had a blank stupid look on his face and arrogantly said, "Well, that is about the most preposterous question you could ask me, young man. How would I be able to do that?"

Mookie responded with, "Bam! In yo' face, partna."

Our efforts were successful. By our third year, we had increased the diverse population of the school by eighty percent, and had chartered several diverse student body organizations. It was interesting that during this fight, I put more time into my studies than I had ever done before but seemed to get lower scores on my papers. This could have put my scholarships in jeopardy. I had a school-sponsored internship since my first year and was excelling in both my job and studies.

After uncovering some questionable practices performed by the school, I seemed to be criticized for my job performance, and received lower grades than I had previously received from some of the professors that I had taken classes with before. I knew my work and school performance were above par, but chose not to fight, because my GPA stayed above the minimum, even with the lower scores. However, Mookie was put on academic probation. He had the attitude that he had tougher fights in the streets, and this too, he would overcome with the God leading him.

I am not certain that God answered his prayer directly, but during the second semester of our third year, Mookie caught two high-ranking members of the staff having sex. After that, all of Mookie's problems disappeared, and his grades increased substantially. The only problem that remained for him was trying to get rid of my stalker sister.

Chapter 4

Tracy met Mookie after visiting me during my first year at divinity school, and the more he tried to push her away, the harder she tried. After Tracy met Mookie, she made the trip from Houston to North Carolina at least twice a month. In an effort to get rid of her, Mookie told her that he had taken a vow of celibacy, and she told him that she would wait indefinitely for him. She constantly brought him presents, which he always refused.

Mookie told me that he did not want to hurt her feelings, or our relationship, but he needed her to stop pushing up on him. Tracy finally got the message when once, during a visit, Mookie brought his "girlfriend" over to meet us. Mookie confided in me that he asked a prospective freshman, that he had recruited, to do him a favor and fake that she was his girlfriend. It worked because Tracy ended her bi-weekly visits; however, this made me question whether Mookie was gay.

After my experience with Ty, my eyes were wide open. I never saw him involved with anyone of the opposite sex. When Sadiq came to visit me, we all three would go out, but Mookie never had a date. However,

Mookie and Sadiq got along well from the first time they met. They were like brothers from another mother. It was funny watching them because they could finish each other's sentences. It seemed like Mookie had more in common with Sadiq, than he did with me. He would call and ask whether his boy was coming up so they could hang. I once asked Sadiq if he minded Mookie always being around, and he stated that he did not mind, as long as we got our quality time apart from Mookie.

Mookie and I shared a lot about our lives, including intimate thoughts about our past, present and future. Mookie wanted to become the pastor of a mega church in the South. His eyes were set on Mississippi because he felt, although the state had a lot of African American pastors, the state lacked a strong African American leadership presence. He envisioned that the next great revolution would arise from Mississippi. Additionally, he wanted to break away from the West Coast because he felt that the ghosts of his past would haunt him there. He rarely kept in touch with his parents or his siblings. Mookie said he did not have any friends outside of his clique, so he really did not leave anyone behind.

The subject of homosexuality came up as we were studying for our Systematic and Philosophical Theology course at Mookie's apartment. I took advantage of the moment to ask him his views about homosexuality. He answered that God created no imperfection, so what God created is good and perfect. I did not understand his answer and thought that he was avoiding the question.

I decided to take this issue head on and said, "I don't think you answered the question I asked."

He said, "Ms. Lady, what do you really want to know?"

"Are you gay?" I asked.

"I don't expect you to believe this, but I have never had sex. I can't officially be labeled as gay or straight."

"Why are you talking in circles?" I asked. "I can show you better than I can tell you."

"What!" I said.

Mookie stood up and started unbuttoning his pants and I said, "No Mookie! What are you doing?"

He continued to pull down his pants and I could see his bulging dick through his underwear.

"Mookie, have you lost your dayum mind! Pull up your pants!" I shouted.

"No, I need to share this with you. I have not shared it with anyone other than my family."

"I am not sure I want you to share this with me," I said softly.

However, I became curious about what he thought he needed to show me. So I just stared as he pulled down his underwear. Based on my limited exposure, Mookie had a nice-sized penis, but I did not see a scrotum. He saw that I was looking at him strangely, so he lifted his penis up. What I saw completely shocked me. Where his balls should have been, was a vagina. I could not utter a sound. My mouth was just wide open for what seemed to be fifteen minutes.

Mookie eventually pulled up his pants and said, "I am what you call intersex. I was born this way. My parents decided that they wanted me to decide whether I wanted to be a girl or boy when I became old enough to make that decision."

"So what are you?" I asked.

"What did you think I was before I showed you my dual parts, Ms. Lady?"

"A fine azz nicca," the old Porchia accidentally blurted out.

"That is what I choose to be. I never felt like a female. I believe that is one of the reasons I joined a gang. I wanted to prove my masculinity."

"Why didn't you get rid of the other?"

"Because my parents always said that God made me special."

"But now you are old enough to make a decision for yourself."

"Now I believe that God makes no mistakes. I was born with a dual genitalia, so that is how I am supposed to be."

"For the first time, I am at a loss for words, Mook."

"I don't expect you to say anything. As I said, no one knows about this but my family. That is the reason I am not in a hurry to get into a relationship with anyone. I don't know how that person would handle it. I don't have a scrotum, so I can't produce kids. I actually have ovaries that can produce eggs. Ms. Lady, that is why I am so sensitive toward you when you are on your period, because I have one too."

"Hey, you have the best of both worlds," I said laughing. Then thought to myself that my statement may have been in bad taste.

However, Mookie quickly responded with, "Yeah, I wished my penis would curve enough so whenever I got horny, I could give myself a good fuck. I'm sorry, Ms. Lady, excuse my French."

"Oh, you think you are that big and good, huh?"

"You saw it fa yo' self. I would prove how good it could be, but I don't want you putting a tracker on a brother, twenty-four seven," Mookie said, while seductively licking his lips.

We both just laughed and I got closer to him and hugged him. While we embraced, I said, "I always knew you were special. And one day, you will find that special woman."

"Just keep this away from your freak sister cuz she seem like she might get turnt up."

I laughed. "It's our secret, Mook."

I looked at Mookie and I saw something different in him that I felt I needed to protect. He had been there as my confidante, protector, and friend over the past two years without me having any idea about his sexual ambiguity, but for him, there seemed to be no ambiguity. He was one of the most confident males I had ever met. His confidence did not come out as cockiness, but just a deep understanding about who he was as a person.

I couldn't quite wrap my mind around understanding how Mookie could be so accepting of his condition. But, I also gained a new appreciation for all of God's children. We debated in class about the morality around homosexuality, bisexuality, and other forms of nonconventional sexuality. As we passionately debated about our thoughts on homosexuality, I questioned who gave man the authority to decide whether what God created is either right or wrong.

I came to the conclusion that, as much as I did not have a choice about my gender, some people do not have a choice about their sexuality. After discovering Mookie's condition, I am more convinced than ever, that God is the ultimate judge, and although He condemns sin, He is accepting of His children that He created in His image.

Chapter 5

During my second year of school, Sadiq had major competition from another guy named Sly. Sly's full name was Sylvester Sly Stone the Second. Mystery and Sweezy produced a little mini-me that was the apple of my eye, whom I spoiled every chance I got. Mystery was on bed rest for most of her pregnancy, so once she delivered Sly, she picked up and pretty much moved in with me. Sweezy did not like being away from them, so he also spent a lot of time with us in my cramped apartment.

I often marveled over the fact that they had a five thousand square foot house in Houston, but preferred staying with me in my seven hundred square foot apartment in Durham. I didn't mind, because Sly made being cramped in a small space worth it. It is amazing how one of God's creations can change the way you view the world. I wanted nothing but the best for Sly, much like Mystery wanted only the best for me.

Sadiq and I behaved more like best friends instead of a couple. We spent a lot of time talking and laughing about life. One evening, we all went out to dinner as we normally did on Saturday night, except this Saturday, we had extra guests, Auntie Char and Tracy. It was normal for Mookie to tag along on our Saturday evening dates, but this was what I classified as a gang of people. Everyone seemed to be giddy, including Sly who was about fifteen months old, going on twenty-five.

He carried on a conversation like a grown person with the exception of his habit of dropping syllables from a person's name. I was not certain whether he had a speech impediment, but he attempted to call me Auntie P, but it came out as Teepee. Sly reminded me a lot of Aunt Hattie because sometimes he would look at me the same way Aunt Hattie would look at me. I did not necessarily believe in reincarnation, but that boy often made me wonder where he got his old soul.

At the end of the meal, the server brought out a cake with a candle on it and I realized that I had forgotten it was Sadiq's birthday. I looked at him and said, "I am so sorry. I have been so busy with work and school, it slipped my mind."

He said, "Don't worry, baby, I understand."

The server set the cake in front of me and I looked at it and it read, Will you marry me? At the bottom of the candle there was a ring with a huge solitaire diamond.

Sly looked at me and started jumping saying, "Say yes, Teepee! Say yes."

I was at a complete loss for words. I just stared and nothing would come out. Everyone's eyes were on me, and I felt my heart racing like it used to do when I was in high school. I later found out that I was experiencing panic attacks.

When I woke up, Sadiq was holding me and telling me to drink some water. I obviously had passed out. When Sly saw I was awake he said, "Teepee, Diq did not mean to kill you. I'm glad you came back."

Everyone fell out laughing, except me. I could not believe Sadiq proposed to me in front of my entire family. I never once thought about us getting married. I knew we were dating, but it did not seem that serious. He never mentioned that he had thoughts of marriage.

"Are you all right, Porchia?" Sadiq asked.

"I am feeling weak and dizzy. I need to go home."

Sweezy rushed over to help Sadiq get me off the floor.

Sweezy said, "Come on, Swoosh. We'll get you home."

Everyone but Sadiq and I had ridden with Sweezy and Mystery in their SUV. I was not looking forward to the ride home alone with Sadiq.

We drove in complete silence until he broke the silence and asked, "What's wrong, Porchia?"

I blurted out, "I never thought we were that serious."

"What do you mean, you never thought we were that serious? We have been dating each other exclusively for almost three years!"

I had never recalled Sadiq raising his voice at me, so I look at him and calmly said, "I know, but we never discussed marriage."

"So what did you think we were leading to, a long extended datingship?"

"I don't know. I never thought about it."

"So when I tell you that I love you, and you tell me that you love me in return, what was that?" "I do love you," I responded.

"But not enough to marry me?"

"I'm just not ready for marriage."

"Is that code for you are not ready for marriage to me?" asked Sadiq.

"That is absurd. If not you, then who?" I asked.

"Well, I think you're the one in the best position to answer that question," said Sadiq.

I became angry with myself because my mind raced back to Ty and the feelings I still had for him.

"I am not ready for marriage to anyone!" I screamed.

"My, aren't we being defensive."

"Yeah, perhaps, but I feel as if I'm being put on trial for a crime I did not commit!"

"Look, Porchia, I want to take our relationship to the next level. I want a wife and a family."

"So it's not me that you want, but you like the idea of having a wife and family."

"I would not have asked you if I did not want you to be my wife, and to have my children!"

"You are way ahead of me, Sadiq, I'm sorry, I am just not ready."

The conversation ended and we drove in silence once again.

When we arrived back at my apartment it was obvious that he was not coming in, so I said, "I'll see you tomorrow."

Sadiq looked at me. "I'll see you when you know what you want."

"So what, you are breaking up with me?"

"I thought we were on the same path, but I see that you need to take a detour. So I will let you decide what you want to do."

Normally Sadiq would have gotten out of the car and opened my door, but I could tell that he was not moving, so I opened my door and looked at him and said, "Goodbye, Sadiq."

When I closed the door, he sped off. I stood there, never imagining that he would have left me standing all alone at night. As I stood there, tears began flowing from my eyes, I felt someone walking up from behind me. I looked back and it was Mookie. He hugged me from behind and said, "It'll be a'ight. One thing I know is that you'll never be pressured into doing something that you don't wanna do. Wait upon the Lord to guide you. He will not lead you in the wrong direction."

I turned around and began crying on his shoulder. I saw a bright light shining in the background. It looked similar to the Light I met at the hospital. I felt a warm feeling rush throughout my entire body. I pulled back from Mookie and said, "Thanks, Mook, I know that you are right. I just feel so bad right now, but I appreciate you being here and saying those words."

"This is where I'm supposed to be at this time."

We stayed outside just hugging without saying anything. The next thing I noticed was Sly running up and pulling on my pant leg saying, "Come in, Teepee, we have to watch the *Minions*."

I had watched that movie with him a million times, but I could not disappoint him, so I would watch Minions a million and one times if it made him happy. Mookie kissed me on the forehead and said he would catch up with me tomorrow. He then picked up Sly and gave him the normal departure routine of throwing him up in the air three times. I took Sly's hand and we walked into the apartment to find Mystery sitting on the sofa looking as if she had lost her best friend.

"Where is Auntie Char and Trace?" I asked.

"We dropped them off at their hotel. I am so sorry, Porchia, I thought you would be excited about the proposal."

"It's all right, Mystery."

"How is Sadiq? I hope he recovers from what you did to him."

Sometimes Mystery had the damndest way with words. The old Porchia would have called her all kinds of names; names which I now would feel bad about even thinking. And to top it off, the old Porchia would have said things that she would not have regretted saying. To be completely honest, at times, I missed the old Porchia.

I quickly recovered from my thoughts about the old Porchia and sharply responded, "We both will get through it, and we appreciate your prayers."

Sweezy came out of the bathroom and saw the look on my face and said, "I need everyone with the last name

Stone to come into the room with me now. It's time for some Stone Family Time."

Sly started protesting and saying that he wanted to watch a movie with me. Sweezy told him that he could watch the movie with me another time. He was about to pout when Sweezy gave him a look that caused him to immediately straighten up. He then came and hugged me and said, "Good night, Teepee. I love you."

"I love you too, snug bug."

I sat down on the sofa with my face in my hands, wondering whether I had made a big mistake by rejecting Sadiq's proposal. Sadiq was pastoring a mega church, working on his doctorate degree, and on his way to achieving both his personal and career goals.

I said to myself, *We are aligned when it comes to our personal beliefs, we get along well, he makes me laugh, he is supportive, he provides great counsel, he is honest, generous, kind, loving, and most of all, he loves the Lord.* Had I made a decision that I would regret for the rest of my life? Then I remembered seeing the Light shining behind me as if it was a sign of approval. I got on my knees and prayed to the Lord. I asked him for wisdom, guidance, and perseverance in doing His will.

Just as I finished praying, Auntie Char called me. She told me she knew that turning down Sadiq's proposal was probably one of the hardest things I have had to do in my life; it was never easy hurting another person, especially one that you love. She went on to say that in the long run, it was the best thing I could have done for the both of us. Living a lie is never the right thing to do. She also commended me for loving Sadiq enough to be honest with him. Those were the words I needed to hear at that time. After hanging up the phone, I thanked God for Chardonnay, and using her as a vehicle to deliver His words to me.

Chapter 6

During my third year of school, I landed a job as an assistant to a producer, Mannie Butchman, on a reality series called *Pimp Ministers*. The show was about former pimps who changed their lives to become ministers. This hit home, since my roots came from Pimp Pastor Charles, who remained a pimp even while being one of the well-respected ministers in Houston.

I started off by managing calendars, appointments, balancing the budget, and running errands for Mannie. Within a few weeks, I was assisting with the script and working closely with the Director, Jim Blumenfield. Blum, as we called him, was a Jewish man that had directed a number of African American shows, but he lacked the knowledge and practical experience as it related to black churches and the pimps who ran them.

I was excited to learn about writing, producing, and directing from some of the experts in the field. I discovered that reality shows did not involve much reality. Practically everything was staged to make a good story. I added some flair to the mix by giving advice about what should happen, everything from robbing the church to extramarital affairs with pastor's wives.

Words like gaffers and grips were totally foreign to me, but became part of my everyday vocabulary. As a result of telling Blum that I did not understand why he made such a big deal about lighting on the set, he made me work closely with the lighting. I gained a first-hand appreciation on how lights could make or break a scene.

I invited Mookie to the set to watch the first live taping of the show. Rechelle, one of the preachers' daughters, caught me in the middle of helping with lighting to ask me whether Mookie was my man. I informed Rechelle that I was busy, but I am certain that Mookie could explain who I was to him. She looked at me up and down then walked away mumbling somewhat loudly, "Bitch, if he is yours, he won't be for long."

Rechelle was a twenty-three-year-old, spoiled brat that was chased by, straight, gay, young and old men, including some of the married preachers on the show. Her father was a billionaire and the biggest pimp of all of the ministers.

Rechelle thought that the world revolved around her, both on and off the set. I saw her lure men in, and then drop them when she was finished. She used them for everything from sex to buying her expensive material objects. I frankly did not think that she was that cute, but she oozed sexuality.

When we were done taping, I noticed that Rechelle was putting her fangs into Mookie, and he seemed to be eating it all up. I didn't worry much because I knew that Mookie had street sense, and would see right through her. When it came down to it, I knew he would not seriously give her a second of his time. But to my dismay, he was laughing like she was the funniest person since Richard Pryor.

I walked over, looked at Mookie, and asked, "Did you enjoy the show?"

"You know I did, Ms. Lady. I saw you doing your thang," Mookie said with a smile on his face.

"Yeah, she does her thang really good, doesn't she?" said Rechelle.

"Not better than you, Reeechelle," I retorted.

Mookie glanced my way with a surprised look on his face.

"So, Mookie, are you ready to go?" I asked.

"No, he is not ready to go until he gets my number," said Rechelle.

"Rechelle, where I am from, ladies wait for men to ask them for their number," I said.

"Well, I am glad we are from different places, Poooor-sha," responded Rechelle.

I was about to go H-town on her when Mookie asked Rechelle if she had a pen. She searched through her Hermes Birkin bag and pulled out her Mont Blanc pen, encrusted with emeralds, rubies, and sapphires and handed it to him. Mookie smiled while checking out the pen, then grabbed her, pulled her closer to him, turned her around, lifted her shirt, and then wrote his number on her back. He grinned and walked away saying in his LA gang banger voice, "Will be waiting fa' yo' call."

I looked at Rechelle and she was grinning from ear-to-ear. I just shook my head, then quickly started walking to catch up with Mookie. When I caught up with him, we were out of the building. I shouted, "Mookie, she ain't no good for you!"

Mookie stopped dead in his tracks and said, "Porchia, what's up? Why you acting all brand new on me?"

"For a good reason!"

"Did you forget who I am and where I am from?"

"That girl is poison!"

"I appreciate your concern, Ms. Lady, but I can handle it. I used to run hoes that put the sk to skeezers."

"I'm sorry. I just know that she is up to no good."

"Come on, let's get out of here. I think you need a Snickers, you were about to turn into Mike Tyson on me."

"Shut up!" I said laughing. "Where are you taking me to eat?"

"Where are you taking me? You just ran away the person that would have paid for the both of us."

"Oh, so you think you got it like that, huh?" I asked.

"Think? You betta be glad I got some religion in me now, cuz I would make a believer out of you," Mookie said with a smirk on his face.

Chapter 7

The first season of *Pimp Ministers* was a hit. Everyone stayed home on Friday nights to make certain they did not miss an episode. And to my surprise, Mookie and Rechelle began dating. She eventually grew on me because I could see that Mookie really liked her. She seemed to like him also, but I was still waiting for the ball to drop. I wondered whether Mookie had told her that he was an intersex person. They seemed to have a blooming happy relationship. I made up my mind that if Mookie was happy, I would be happy for him. I knew that he was also adhering to the Christian principles, so he probably was not engaging in sex.

I went to work one day and Mannie told me he needed to speak with me. I went into the office and he looked at me and asked, "So do you think you could talk your freak friend into becoming part of our show?"

I was not sure what or whom he was talking about so I said, "What friend?"

"You know, your friend with the pussy and the dick. Rechelle told me about it and I think it would be great for second season ratings."

I was dumbfounded. *How could she betray Mookie like that?*

I looked at Mannie and said, "I'm sorry, I'm not feeling well. I need to leave."

I went back to my desk, grabbed my purse, and headed home. I did not know what I was going to do. How would I tell Mookie that the woman he trusted, betrayed him? I played over the conversation over and over in my head. I did not want to hurt Mookie. I knew all too well what it felt like to be betrayed. Within three months of breaking up with Sadiq, he was engaged to another woman. He must have had her in a holding pattern until I told him that I was not ready for marriage. How was I to tell Mookie that Rechelle was only using him as a means of getting paid?

When I returned to work the next day, Mannie asked me if I had gotten the opportunity to speak with Mookie about joining the show. He went on talking about how it would be a win-win for everybody involved. I tuned him out until he said, "Porchia, what do you think?"

"I think I feel a migraine coming on, and that I won't be able to stay here today."

"Porchia, are you okay? That is two days in a row. I need you here."

"Well, could you please let me do my work and stop asking about Mookie?" I said.

"Okay, grab your tablet. There are a few things I need to tell you about," said Mannie.

"Okay. I will be there in a minute."

****

I knew that I could not put off talking to Mookie any longer about what his scheming girlfriend was up to. I left him a message telling him that we needed to speak right away. Mookie and I made arrangements to meet at his apartment after I left work. I rehearsed what I was going to say to him. Nothing in my classes taught me how to share bad information with someone, about a person that they cared for. I knew that it was right to practice compassion, but how compassionate could one be letting someone know that they are being used. I thought about telling Mannie to ask Mookie himself, but I did not want Mookie to think I was part of the scheme.

When I arrived, Mookie surprised me with a prepared dinner of tacos and margaritas. I really did not drink anything but wine these days, but I thought I would try a couple of margaritas. I needed some liquid courage and almost asked Mookie to just give me straight shots of tequila.

As we began to discuss potential subjects for our senior project, I asked Mookie whether he had any plans after graduation. He told me that he had applied for grad school at Columbia, but probably would be pursuing other interests, that he wanted to discuss with me. This conversation was all a surprise to me because I thought Mookie's eyes were on a mega church in Mississippi. He informed me that he had been discussing with Rechelle, the possibility of joining the show.

"You mean Rechelle knows about your condition?"

"I don't have a condition, but Rechelle knows that I am intersex."

"Why didn't you tell me?" I asked.

"I didn't think it was CNN worthy."

"It is! I have been upset for two days thinking that Rechelle had betrayed your confidence. That is why I told you that we needed to talk."

"Look, Porchia, I think I am in love with Rechelle and she says that she is in love with me. We have not had sex, but I wanted her to know about my sexuality because that would be important information to someone who has chosen to become involved with me."

"Yeah, but why would you want to put yourself as a spectacle for the entire world to see?"

"I have run away from this long enough. I have done things to prove that I was okay with myself. When actually, I was not. I was running away from who I am. I have come to realize that my sexuality does not define me. It is up to me to define who I am. I don't mind the world knowing who I am. I want to face the demons that have been haunting me since birth. Even coming to seminary school was based on my sexual anatomy. I felt it would be a safe haven for me. I thought if I surrounded myself in an environment where people were kind and compassionate, I would find understanding and acceptance. I quickly learned that seminary school was only a mirror of what we find within our society. I now love myself enough to put it all out there. And if loving me is wrong, I don't want to be right."

I applauded and said, "Nice dissertation, Mr. Davis."

Mookie laughed and said, "Ms. Lady, just eat your tacos before I attack you and them."

Chapter 8

Everyone around me had plans for their lives after graduation. I was drifting about without knowing exactly what I was going to do. Mannie offered me the position as Creative Director for the show, but I felt that I had much more to offer. I gained a lot of experience working on the show, but I did not feel it was the direction that God wanted me to go. I did not share the same excitement or zeal that everyone else around me demonstrated. Although I was a creator for the general direction of the show, I felt disconnected from my spiritual being.

Mookie became an instant hit on the show. He was given the position of Assistant Pastor at Rechelle's father's church, which made the story line even better. We manufactured a story plot that included Mookie taking over, as pastor of Rechelle's father's church, with Rechelle being the mastermind behind the hostile takeover. The plot surrounding Mookie revealing that he was an intersex person really intrigued a lot of folks. Once he revealed his sexuality, Mookie gave Rechelle the freedom to use both of his anatomies in any manner she decided. And she took the liberty to do that on air, by sometimes engaging in oral sex and enjoying both anatomies. For me, the show became more of a porn show, which was borderline blasphemy, being depicted by people claiming to be led by God.

I often voiced my concern with Mookie about how the show was not a good representation of how Christians should behave. I told him that we should be demonstrating behavior that when we did reach heaven God would say, "Job well-done." Mookie told me that what he was doing was strictly entertainment. He went on to say that actors would be unemployed if they only accepted jobs that reflected their personal beliefs or lifestyles. God understood his heart, and that he accepted Him as his Savior is what distinguished him as a Christian, not his job. And while he was popular, he was going to get paid for it. Whereas, I felt that my job was an extension of me, and should be reflective of me living a Godly life. Otherwise, I felt that I would be selling my soul to the devil.

I had an internal battle with my spiritual being during the entire second season. When Mannie pressured me into making a decision on whether I would take the job, I turned him down. Mookie begged me to stay and turn the show into something that I could be proud to represent. I told Mookie that the show had gone too far for me to be able to interject my creative thoughts now. I thought my ideas would only bring the ratings down, because they were headed for another smash season and could possibly see an Emmy award soon. Either way, remaining to work there would be no-win situation, so it was time for me to move on.

During the summer semester, before my last year, I decided to take a break and spend some time in Houston to reflect on the next stage of my life. I felt that I knew more about God and myself, but it did not seem that attending seminary school had prepared me for the next phase of my life. I realized that I needed the ability to maintain a lifestyle with some level of comfort. After all, my molesting, child abusing, father's life insurance proceeds would not last a lifetime.

During these moments, I really missed speaking with Sadiq to get his input. I found that he was very thoughtful and acted not only as a guidance counselor, but also served as my spiritual advisor. Previously, I had called him and told him it was important for me to speak with him. He never returned my call. Based on that, I think his message to me was very clear; he did not want anything further to do with me. I was glad to be headed back to Houston because I knew that Auntie Char would be a great person to openly discuss my feelings.

When I arrived in Houston, it was great just to smell the air. When Mystery picked me up, I demanded that she took me to Frenchy's. I had searched up and down Durham but could not find good fried chicken.

During the drive, Mystery was not as talkative as normal. I could tell that something was bothering her. She probably was mad because Sweezy had put his foot down about something that she wanted to do, and he did not want. Mystery wanted everything her way or no way at all. I figured I would let her talk and not question her about whatever it was that had her in a funk.

We were at Frenchy's and as I was biting down on my juicy chicken leg Mystery blurted out, "Chardonnay is back in the hospital."

"What! I just spoke with her last week, how long has she been in the hospital?"

"We rushed her to the hospital three days ago."

"Why didn't you call me?"

"Because we knew that you were going through finals and that you would be here soon."

"So what is going on?"

"The leukemia returned and it is really aggressive. They don't think a bone marrow transplant will help this time."

"So what are you saying, Mystery?"

"I am not a doctor, but I don't think it is good."

I got up and said, "Come on. Drive me there now! You should have told me when you picked me up from the airport!"

When I walked into Auntie Char's room, she had tubes coming out from everywhere. However, when she saw me, I saw her eyes smile. I quickly walked over and said, "So I guess you wanted a place where you could be by yourself. You should have told me, I could have stayed at Mommy Dearest."

She squeezed my hand when I said that. It was a joke between us that I called Mystery, Mommy Dearest. My eyes began tearing up seeing her laying like that. To fight back my tears, I said, "Would you like to pray?"

Auntie Char squeezed my hand, so I began saying a prayer. When I finished, I could see tears rolling down Auntie Char's face. I asked, "Auntie Char, I did not mean for my prayer to be that bad. I guess all that money I am paying for school is not helping me with my prayer skills."

I could see that she started smiling again. I looked around the room to see if there was something I could put near her bed. I found a big comfortable chair and dragged it over. I looked up, and Mystery walked in.

"Hi, Sister. How is my favorite sister feeling today? It seems like you have more color to you today than yesterday."

I often wondered where Mystery's mind was. My little brother demonstrated more common sense than Mystery did at times. I rolled my eyes at Mystery, and looked at Auntie Char and said, "Well, we'll have time to catch up on some television shows. I will make certain that we watch my favorite show, Pimp Ministers."

I never discussed my real feelings with them about the show because they all liked it, and they were so proud that I was working on the show. We were talking to Auntie Char for about fifteen minutes before Mystery said that she had to attend to some business. She asked me whether I wanted her to take me to get one of their spare cars so I could have transportation. I told her that I would stay with Auntie Char until she had taken care of her business.

It turned out that Auntie Char was in a lot of pain, and they kept her heavily medicated. I talked to her for a little while before she drifted off to sleep. I informed her nurse that I would like to speak with the doctor when he was available. I guess I drifted off to sleep because I felt a tap on my shoulder. When I looked up, it was Demetrius Turner. He was a senior on the boys' basketball team when I was a freshman.

"Well, isn't this a pleasant surprise? How are you doing, Porchia?"

I stood up, hugged him, and said, "Hey, D-Man. What are you doing here?"

"I heard that you wanted to speak with me."

"No, you ain't no doctor now?"

"Yes, I am now Dr. D-Man," he said laughing.

"Wow, so are you Auntie Char's doctor?"

"Yes, I am Chardonnay's doctor."

"I am impressed. I did not know that you were that smart."

"Ha, I see you still have a way with words."

"What I remember about you is that you skipped class, drank, and smoked weed all day long. I just knew your teachers had to be passing you because you still played ball despite your grades."

"And I remember you being a hot-headed freshman when I was in high school. I don't know how you would know anything about what I did or did not do. So what does all of that mean, Porchia?"

"Okay, sorry. I am just surprised. It's nice to see you."

"So what have you been doing these days?"

"Well, I will be in my last year at Duke Divinity School this fall."

"The girl that cussed out people who looked at her, in what she felt was the wrong way, goes to a divinity school? Now that is a funny one."

"Hey, I have stop judging you, so don't judge me!"

He laughed and said, "No, I will leave that to your Master."

"So what is going on with my aunt?"

"I did not see your name on the privacy form that she signed. Let me check to see if it is okay to discuss her medical information with you. I'll be right back."

When he left the room, I was still in amazement. I could not believe Demetrius was a doctor. He was the one that should have been voted "least likely to succeed" because he cut more classes than he attended. I thought he attended the community college and played basketball there. Evidently, I had it all twisted. And he grew into a fiiine man. When he returned I was deep in thought about him. I jumped when he said, "Porchia."

"So can we talk?"

"Yes, your name was on the form. You don't have the same last name as your mother."

"Yes, that is a long story. So what is the deal with my aunt?"

"Well, she is in the last stage. What we are trying to do now is keep her as comfortable as possible?"

"Did she just go from being okay to being bad?"

"No, she has been sick for a while. We have been giving her all types of treatments."

"She did not say anything to me."

"Chardonnay is a very strong woman. She did not want anyone to feel sorry for her. As I understand it, she had been working until she collapsed at her job."

"What?"

"Yeah, one of her employees rushed her to the hospital."

"I am so upset right now. Someone could have told me because although she is always in my prayers, I could have been specifically praying about this particular condition."

"Well, does your God put a time limit on when he answers prayers?"

"My God?"

"I'm sorry. I don't mean no disrespect."

"You don't believe in God?"

"I neither believe, nor do I disbelieve. I believe in things that can be proven. Existence of God can't be proved or disproved."

"Well, Demetrius, my life is living proof of His existence. And there are some other things that I could point out that proves that He lives."

"I would love to continue this discussion, but I have some rounds to make. Is it possible for us to continue this discussion over dinner?"

"Hey, I love living a textbook moment and teaching a person a thing or two. Most definitely."

Demetrius took my number and said that he would call me to make arrangements for dinner. I told him that I would be looking forward to it.

When he left, I wondered how could a person whose life has turned around so drastically believe that everything happens is circumstantial, or that it happened based solely on one's own abilities. Yes, I was definitely interested in speaking with Demitrius about his life and his beliefs.

I stayed with Auntie Char just holding her hand as she drifted in and out of sleep until Mystery came back a few hours later. Mystery said that she had some interviews to conduct at Aunt Hattie's retreat within the next hour. Unless I was going to be staying all night, this was the best time for her to take me to get one of the cars. So I kissed Auntie Char, told her that I loved her, and that I would be back as soon as possible. She seemed to understand, because once again, she squeezed my hand.

Mystery and I did not engage in conversation on the way to her house to pick up the car. I was still upset that she did not think that she should have called me when Auntie Char was initially admitted to the hospital. When we arrived at Mystery's house, she handed me the keys to the Range Rover.

"Sweezy is in the house waiting for you," she said and then pulled off in the car. I know that Mystery was upset about Chardonnay, but I thought that she was still acting strange.

Chapter 9

I walked up to Mystery and Sweezy's door and rang the doorbell. The nanny, Ausprey, opened the door and greeted me with a hug. She was always so chipper and talkative and must have asked me a hundred questions before Sweezy walked in and said, "Ok, Ausprey, don't run her away before she can settle in."

Sweezy then walked over, gave me a wet kiss on my forehead and said, "I missed you Swoosh!"

"I missed you too. Where is my snug bug?"

"He was too cranky. I told him that he had to take a nap if he wanted you to come. So he ran to his bed and now he is knocked out. Come and talk with your dad for a while."

Sweezy led me to the family room where he sat in his chair and I took a seat on the ottoman in front of him. "So, Daddy, what is wrong with Mommy Dearest?"

"You wrong, Swoosh, for calling Queen that. She is really taking Chardonnay's sickness hard. Ever since she found out that Chardonnay is dying, she has been withdrawn. I was so happy that you were coming. I thought perhaps you could help her out of this funk. It is like she is in a depression or something."

"Really? I did not think they were that close."

"Perhaps not as close as you two are, but I know that she loves her. And another part of it, I think that she thought after she had the bone marrow process for Chardonnay, that she would be cured forever. I think she took for granted that Chardonnay would be living a long healthy life. Now that she is dying, she regrets the time that she did not spend with her."

"I didn't understand why I was so drawn to spend the summer here, but it is all clear now. This is where God has directed me to be. I hope I can fulfill my purpose, whatever that is."

"Well, I am glad that God directed you to be here. We need you, Swoosh."

I leaned over and hugged Sweezy and said, "We all need each other."

"Yes, and we would love if you stayed over here with us," said Sweezy.

"I had not planned on it, but since Auntie Char is at the hospital, I don't really want to stay at the house by myself."

"Good, it is settled. I already arranged for your bags to be brought to the guest room next to Sly's."

"Oh, you just knew your speech would work and that I would agree to stay here."

"Not really. But I knew that you would want to be close to Sly."

"You just know me too well. Well, I am going to go shower and take a quick nap while my snug bug is sleeping."

"Okay. You know Ms. Marvelle is here to cook anything that you want to eat. She has been waiting on you."

"Okay, let me go speak to her before I go clean up."

****

After taking my shower, I decided to go lay with Sly. He was still fast asleep. I cuddled up next to him and fell out. I woke up to something wet on my cheek. It was Sly, slobbering his kisses all over my face. I jumped up and started tickling him. He laughed until he started crying.

I stopped and hugged him and said, "I missed you, Snug Bug."

"I missed you too, Teepee."

"Have you been a good young man?"

"Yes, Teepee. I listen to daddy, mommy, Msprey, Msvel, and Teechar. I say prayers before eating, I read my bible, and pray every night before going to bed."

"That's my Snug Bug."

"Are you going to sleep in my bed, Teepee?"

"No, but I will be sleeping in the room next door. Will that work?"

"Yes, Teepee, I love you."

"Teepee loves you more. Are you ready to eat?"

He started jumping on the bed and screaming, "Yes! Yes! Yes!"

My phone started ringing and it was Penny. I decided to let it go to voicemail so I could get Sly ready for dinner.

I listened to my voicemail from Penny after I settled Sly at the table for his dinner. Penny was crying and I could hardly understand what she was saying. I immediately called her back and she answered saying, "Pocahontas, Brother is hurt and in the hospital."

"What happened sweetie?"

"He had an accident while playing basketball and was knocked unconscious."

"Where are you?"

"I am at Aunt Verdie's."

"Where is Ty?"

"I saw it on the news. No one is saying anything to me. They act as if I am a child that would not understand. I looked up information on my iPad and it said he was at a hospital in Philadelphia."

"Okay, sweetie, I will call and try to find out some more information. I will call you back."

I researched and found out which hospital he was in and tried to find out about his condition, but I could not get any information over the phone. I did not have anyone's number but Jinn's. She probably did not have much contact with anyone from the team since she divorced Raheem, but I thought it was worth a try.

I called Jinn and had to listen to her ramble on and on about school, how she finally felt independent, and blah, blah, blah. She finally paused and I was able to ask if she knew any way to find out information about Ty's condition. She told me she was still in contact with the Manager of Team Relations and that she could call him to get the scoop.

Within the hour, Jinn called me back and told me that he had a concussion, but was improving. The management team was limiting his contact because they wanted him to get the needed rest to get back on the court soon. I told Jinn to please get word to him to call Penny. Jinn was totally unaware that Ty was guardian to his little sister, but she promised that she would take care of it right away.

I called Penny an hour later, and she told me that Ty had called her. She thanked me for making sure that he initiated contact with her. I asked her whether she had any plans for tomorrow. She told me no, so I asked her to speak to her Aunt Verdie.

Aunt Verdie came to the phone and said, "Well, hello Porchia. How are you baby?"

"I am fine Ms. Verdie. And how are you doing?"

"I am still kicking and I have my good mind chile."

I chuckled and said, "Well, that is good to hear. And how is Poo Man?"

"Poo Man is still working as an offshore man. He is in and out of town. Seems like that boy spends more time on the water than he spends at home. I have given up on having a grandchild. But I am glad I have Penny to spend time with me. She is such a charming child."

"Yes, she is great. That is what I am calling about. Is it possible for me to take her out tomorrow afternoon?"

"Of course baby. What time?"

"About three o'clock."

"Okay, that will work."

I then called Tracy and asked her what was she doing tomorrow. She excitingly said that she had no plans. So I told her we were going on an outing with our brothers and sisters, Penny, and Sly. She started objecting and I told her that we have to invest in the young ones because they are our future. I think she did not want to listen to my rant, so she begrudgingly agreed.

After hanging up with Tracy, Demetrius called and asked whether he could take me out to dinner tomorrow. I told him I had plans for tomorrow, but would love for him to join in on the plans. I filled in Demetrius on what I had planned, and he agreed.

During the conversation, he revealed that he was a single father raising a twelve year-old son. He said that his ex-wife left them when his son, Colin, was only two months old. She suffered badly from postpartum depression, and started doing drugs. Eventually, she became hooked on crack, and abandoned him and their infant son.

Demetrius thought it would be great for his son to meet other children his age. According to him, he wanted his child to grow up in a very different environment than what he was subjected to. Therefore, he placed his son in a private school with a minimum number of people of color. Now he was worried that his son was not as well-rounded as he probably should be for a child his age. He said his son lacked the ability to deal with other black children, and seemed to lack common street sense. He feared that his son would be a target if he did not learn how to appropriately interact with other black children.

We took off on a field trip, which consisted of seven kids ranging from age four to thirteen. We started off at the zoo, then went to the Children's Museum, and ended the evening at the Downtown Aquarium where we also grabbed food to eat. The evening was successful. Although Colin was a little different, all the kids got along well. They all took special interest in taking care of Sly since he was the youngest in the crowd, especially Penny and Colin.

I noticed that Penny and Colin were getting real chummy. They seemed to have more in common, since they both attended predominantly white, private schools. What was even more interesting was watching Tracy throw herself at Demetrius, and him trying to fight off her blatant advances. To the point she was undressing him with her eyes, and he was insinuating that he was gay. At different times, they both approached me and asked me what was wrong with the other one. Demetrius let me know straight out that he had no interest in Tracy; whereas, Tracy let me know that she would not stop pursing Dr. Demetrius Frank.

Tracy was a beautiful woman, but had a difficult time keeping a man. I attributed that to her not completely healing after our father sexually abused her. She received years of counseling, but I am not certain it helped. She did not like the men that were interested in her; however, the minute a guy showed that they were not interested in her, she would chase him to the ends of the earth.

About three years ago, she dated an Indian friend of mine, Ravi. That eventually sizzled when Ravi started attending Georgetown, and he found another love interest. Tracy stalked him and his girlfriend for about a year. I attempted to talk with her about it, but she told me repeatedly that she knew Ravi loved her. She was relentless until Ravi put a restraining order against her.

However, despite the non-love connection between Demetrius and Tracy, the evening left everyone exhausted, but with smiles, especially the children. When I dropped Penny back at Aunt Verdie's, she asked whether she could spend a night with me. I told her that I would talk to Aunt Verdie to arrange a date for her to spend a night soon. I was unsure about how long Penny would be staying with Aunt Verdie. I was actually surprised that she was in Houston. I knew that Ty had hired a nanny for her. I would have to get the scoop from Ty on why Penny was not at home in Birmingham with her nanny.

Later that night, Demetrius called me and told me that I still owed him a date. I questioned him about whether he liked men or women. He said, "That is the only way I know how to get away from an aggressive woman."

"Well, you better be glad that it worked, because normally that would not have deterred my sister, The Shark Lady."

Demitrius laughed and said, "Yeah, I could tell that she is a man-eater."

"So what is the problem, you don't feel like getting eaten?"

"Only by someone I choose."

"Oh, I see you're a choosey lover."

"Well if it was my choice, it would be someone like you. So what's up with you? Are you seeing someone?"

"No time for that in my life right now."

"Yeah, that has been my line too. But look, I have to help Colin with some homework. He is attending a summer academic camp and has a project that I promised I would help him with. So if it is okay, I will call you to set up a date for later on in the week."

"Okay, sounds good. Before hanging up, how is Auntie Char?"

"About the same."

'Okay, thanks, will speak with you later."

"You bet. Have a good night," Demetrius responded.

"Goodnight!"

Chapter 10

I went to Houston to try to determine the next steps in my life, but I became inundated with family issues, spending time with Auntie Char, my brothers and sisters, Penny, and Demetrius. However, Demetrius helped me determine the subject matter of my senior project. We spent a lot of time talking about God and proof that He exists.

After Auntie Char, who once was an agnostic, walked out of the hospital in what seemed like a complete remission, I decided to write my senior project around a theme involving the views of agnostics. I titled the project, *The Intangible God who Delivers Tangible Benefits*. I dedicated my research to people who converted from either atheists or agnostics to believing in God, and what happened after their transformation.

Once I returned to school, I worked hours, days, and weeks perfecting research, and documenting everything from people who went from crack to stardom, to people on their deathbed who walked away with a complete recovery. This was a very moving subject for me because I also met The Light and had converted from atheism to Christianity.

However, the most compelling stories came from those who were celebrities in the public's eyes. I attempted to keep everyone anonymous, but because I shared intimate details of their stories, it was evident who some of my subjects were.

I received a letter from Christian Times Publishing advising me that they were happy to represent me as one of their premier new authors. I had not submitted my information to anyone, so I called them to ask what the letter was about. I eventually found out that my academic research advisor, who supervised my senior project, sent my work to them.

I was on a whirlwind during my last year of school. I was offered a job by Christian Time Inc. before graduating and started working on my second book. My plate was extremely full because not only was I a fulltime student, I was busy still assisting Mookie with recruiting female, minority, and underprivileged students. I wanted more than anything for this to be our legacy when we left school.

A lot of the work fell on me because Mookie was busy playing out his celebrity status on Pimp Ministers. It was amazing to watch how his world changed. We could not go anywhere without someone recognizing him from the show. He took it all in gracefully, because despite all of the stardom, he was still Mookie.

I looked around at everything that was happening so quickly, but I think the proudest moment during my last year is when Demetrius called me and asked me whether

I would come to his baptism. We talked for hours on end, but I never imagined that I had convinced Demetrius that there was a God, and He existed today through his Spirit.

I must admit that during this time, Demetrius and I had a strange relationship. Neither of us were seeing anyone, but I can't say that we were involved with each other either. We never once shared any intimacy outside of the deep discussions that we had about God and life, but we stayed in constant contact. I was there for him, as much as he was there for me.

When I went to Demetrius' baptism, everyone treated us as if we were a couple. Later on that night, he and I went out to eat and the proverbial elephant in the room raised its old, ugly, wrinkled trunk again. Demitrius looked at me and said, "So what are we doing, Porchia?"

"Eating," I responded.

"No, I am talking about us. Is there an us?"

I really hated being backed into a corner. Everything was going so well between us. I thought to myself, *Why did he have to bring this subject up in our time of celebration!*

"Do we have to label what we have? I enjoy the time we spend together," I said.

"I do too. But I would like to know if we are moving toward something more tangible."

"Look, Demetrius, I don't want to hold you back from pursuing anything or anyone that you may be interested in."

"I don't want to pursue anyone. I am interested in only you. I am trying to figure out if you feel the same way?"

What am I going to say? I don't want to let another good man just slip through my fingers, but I don't know how I feel. I know that I enjoy what we do have at this time. But I don't know if it is something I want forever. Honesty is the best policy, Porchia.

"Demetrius, I don't want to lose what we have. So whatever we need to do, to ensure that we don't lose it, let's do it."

I said to myself, *where the hell did that come from?*

"I am glad to hear you say that, Porchia. I just need to know that there is no one else and that we are exclusive to each other."

As long as he does not come out with a proposal or a ring, I can handle it.

"I only want to see you, Demitrius."

He leaned forward to kiss me. I feared where this might lead, but I went along with the long passionate kiss. For some reason, I had a flashback to the first time Sadiq kissed me, and where it landed us. I did not want another crash landing. I pulled back and asked, "Demetrius, you know that I don't engage in premarital sex right?"

"No. I was not sure. But now I know."

"Well, is that going to be a problem for you?"

"It has not been yet. And I know that you will be well worth the wait."

"Well, I think it is important to be honest at all times. If it does become a problem, do you promise we'll talk about it?"

"Porchia, I don't think that it will be a problem because I see something more permanent in our future anyway."

I think I sighed out loud because he gave me a strange look. I recovered and said, "It has been one eventful day. I'm exhausted. I am ready to call it a night."

"Sure, I understand. I'll take you home."

When we arrived back at Auntie Char's house, I thanked him for a lovely evening and told him I was so proud that he had accepted Jesus into his life. He told me that he owed everything to me and reached over to kiss me again. I made it a short one and told him, "Look don't start nothing, and there will be nothing." He laughed and got out of the car to open my door. He walked me up to the door and I gave him a peck on the lips and said, "Goodnight."

When I got in the house, I sat on the sofa wondering, *What was I doing? I knew that I enjoyed Demetrius' company, his conversation, and being in his presence. But was I ready for another relationship? How does one carry on an intimate relationship with someone, when the only person you really desire to get to know more deeply is God?*

I loved my family and friends, but God came before all others. I don't think that men are able to fully and completely accept that from someone they feel is important to them, or that they love.

Although I had not yet completed my second book, I could not wait to start my third book, which would be titled, *Love and Intimacy vs. Godliness.* Perhaps through deep introspection, I would understand how I could balance both.

Chapter 11

One night I was up late working on a paper for one of my classes and True Entertainment came on and announced that NBA sensation, Tyrese Gamble was getting married. I looked up and there was Ty all hugged up with some chic that reminded me of the ol' skool Angie Stone with the fro and all.

Something stirred up in me and I wanted to pick up the phone and cuss him out. I don't know where this reaction came from, because I had really not spoken with Ty. We had only talked in passing a few times, and it usually had something to do with Penny. He seemed to have given up on having a relationship with me after I turned him down repeatedly.

I shook off the feelings and went back to working on my paper. I was in deep thought about what I was going to write next when I received a text message from Demetrius telling me that he was just thinking about me. I smiled, and somehow, he gave me the motivation I needed to finish my paper; the last one I had to complete before graduating.

I found myself drifting and thinking about the last four years of my life. So much had happened in such a short period of a time. Sadiq and I broke up, and I started a relationship with another loving, supportive and kind man. I had a brother born who I adored, and who was growing like a weed. I had an aunt who defied all odds and beat leukemia. I was involved in creating one of the number one shows on television. And now, I was being featured in *Essence* Magazine as one of the up and coming black theologians in America. But most importantly, my love, respect and honor for God had grown substantially over the past four years.

A person looking in at a review of my life might think that what had happened over the last four years was quite impressive. But something was still missing from my life. I started thinking that perhaps it was my relationship with Mystery that was still lacking.

Although we spent a lot of time together over the last four years, I am not certain I can say that we were as close as we should be. I still could not confide in her the way that I confided in Aunt Hattie, Auntie Char, or Sweezy. I don't think I accepted her as my mother, despite the fact that I wanted to so badly. I loved her and accepted her limitations, as well as her abilities. However, I wanted someone I could relate to as a mother, and Mystery's and my relationship had not risen to that level. It was almost like I saw her as the big sister that I dearly loved.

I pondered whether I had forgiven Mystery after lying about being my mother, but I knew that I had long gotten over that. I knew that forgiving was the first part of the healing process. It was as if I conjured her up because she called me while I was deep in thought.

It was after midnight when she called, which I thought was odd, but she said she knew I was up, and she just wanted to check in to see how thing were going. I could tell by the meekness that I heard in her voice, something was wrong. After allowing her to tell me about what was going on for the last week with Sly, Sweezy, Auntie Char, and Aunt Hattie's Retreat, she finally said, "I have breast cancer."

My first thought was, *Lord, we have just gotten through a rough ordeal with Auntie Char, please don't bring this upon me and our family again.*

"How long have you known?"

"I learned the day that Chardonnay went into the hospital."

"Why did you not say anything?"

"You had enough on your plate with school and worrying about Chardonnay. I did not want to place that extra burden on you worrying about me. I am not certain how much time I have left now. I am afraid that you might haunt me after death, if I did not to tell you. And I need to kick it with Aunt Hattie peacefully," Mystery said and chuckled.

"Mystery, there are a lot of treatments for breast cancer."

"Porchia, I have explored many different options, and have gone through various treatments. The biopsies revealed that I would have to have double mastectomy, accompanied by radical treatment. The doctors were honest and revealed that it probably had spread throughout my body. I don't want Sweezy to go through the pain with me, or have him exposed to seeing me without breasts. I want him to remember the whole me. The me that he fell in love with. Nor do I want my little man knowing that Mommy is dying. I decided to go through this alone. Well, not really alone, God and Aunt Hattie have been with me the entire time."

For the first time, I did not feel like it was all about Mystery. She spoke about how she would be honored if I helped Sweezy raise Sly, and be there as much as possible to help Sweezy accept her death. She told me that she did not expect me to put my life on hold, but to pitch in whenever I could. She asked me to pray with her that everyone would be okay after she left.

I assured her that she was not going anywhere soon, so we needed to concentrate on living, not dying. Mystery said she was just trying to be realistic and plan for all of us as much as she could before leaving. She told me that she had not discussed her diagnosis with Sweezy and wanted me to pray that he had the strength to handle her illness, and eventual death.

When I hung up the phone, I cried, and cried for hours. I prayed to God to allow us time to become mother and daughter. I told Him that it would be unfair of Him to take away Sly's mother at such an early age. And even more unfair, that Sweezy would have to deal with the death of losing another person whom his world revolved around. He almost gave up on life when Chanti died, so I did not know how he could survive Mystery's death.

During my period of crying and praying, God revealed to me that time waits for no one. He told me that we must make the best of the time that is given to us. It was during this time, I realized that we could take no day, no hour, no minute, no second for granted.

For the remainder of my last semester, I shuttled between Durham and Houston trying to be supportive for Mystery, Sly, and Sweezy. Chardonnay also put her life on hold to help Mystery, Sweezy and Sly. Sweezy convinced Mystery to do everything possible to win the fight against breast cancer; so she eventually elected to have a double mastectomy and chemotherapy. She lost her battle with breast cancer six months, and two days after she confided in me that she had cancer.

She fought to the very end, but not once did she whimper or complain, even though everyone around her could clearly see that she was in pain. During this time, my mother stayed upbeat and positive until she took that last breath. Before going, she had a speech for all of us. We let her speak without any interruptions.

She said to Auntie Char, "I feel so blessed that you sought me out. You gave me the gift of loving unconditionally. We had our problems, but we were eventually able to live and love each other as sisters. Keep up the battle with leukemia, because you will win that war. I am entrusting the legacy of Auntie Hattie's

Retreat to you. She reminded me a lot of you, a strong woman. I wish you had the same opportunity that I had, to be raised by her. I know she would have loved you, and you would have loved her in return. Just as I truly love you."

She then turned to me and said, "Porchia, I can't wait until you have children of your own. There is no greater love than the love that a mother has for her child. You were my very first love. I love both you and Sly with all of my being. And I am so proud of the woman that you have become. I wish I had more time to show you how much you both mean to me. Please take care of my two men for me. They will need you more than ever now. And take care of yourself. You need to understand that it is all right to put your needs before others at times. You should also be glad to know that I have made peace with the Lord, and have turned my life over to Him. So I will see you there my first love. And don't cry for me. I want you to celebrate my memory and my life."

She began gazing at Sweezy as if she was at a loss for words, and for the first time, tears began gushing down her face. She said, "You are the best husband, father, mate, and friend that anyone could ever have. If I lived forever, that would not be enough time to show you how much I love you. Every day, every moment, I spent with you was precious. I always felt safe with you by my side. I knew that together, we could battle anything. Not once did you disappoint me with anything that you ever did. You always put your family's needs before your own.

When I leave, try to be strong. Carry on for Sly's sake. He will need you more than ever now. With you as his role model, he will grow into the man that I will be proud of. I love you baby, more than you could ever imagine. Please do whatever is necessary for you to live life and be happy."

We all stood there silently in tears, holding my mother's hand until she took her last breath. When I saw that her breathing had changed I shouted out, "Mother, I love you!"

By the time we left the hospital, Sweezy was a beaten man, but was attempting to be strong and fighting for Sly's sake. That evening we all went home with Sweezy to be his support when he told Sly that his mommy was gone.

We knew that this was hard on all of us, but especially Sweezy. I had to take over because Sweezy was having a difficult time talking about Mystery's death. Later that night, I found Sweezy in his office with a bottle of Remy just bawling like a baby. He reminded me of the broken Sweezy that I witnessed at Chanti's funeral. When he saw me he said, "I don't know how I will make it, Swoosh."

I responded, "With God and your family by your side."

Looking back, this period of time was just a blur to me and graduation from Duke Divinity School was insignificant. Everything was so surreal. I knew that I had stories to tell, so I kept writing through this difficult time. My third book hit number one on the NY *Times*

Best Seller's List. At this time, Christian Times Inc. decided that they would like me to host a radio talk show. I agreed with the condition that I would be allowed to broadcast from Houston. I knew I had to be close to Sweezy and Sly, not only for their sake, but for my sake also.

Although Auntie Char and I still lived together, I spent most of my days and nights at Sweezy's. Sweezy tried to convince me that he had it all under control, and with the help of Ausprey and Ms. Marvelle, I did not need to watch him and Sly like a hawk. However, I did not want any other woman having more of an influence on my brother than me. By this time, Sly was in kindergarten and very impressionable. Nothing against Ausprey or Ms. Marvelle, but they were not kinfolk, as Aunt Hattie would have said.

Chapter 12

During this period in my life, Demetrius was as supportive as any partner could be. He even looked into alternative medicines for Mystery, but nothing worked. He was the person constantly in my ear saying, "Don't give up. You know what happened with Chardonnay."

Once Mystery went on to her heavenly home, he was the person that gave me constant encouragement that I would get through this rough patch. He attempted to get me to go see a grief counselor, but I assured him that God was my counselor, and that God and I would work it out together.

I did not once think that losing Mystery would have such an effect on me. I remember losing Aunt Hattie and thinking that this was the worst thing that could happen to me, next to losing Chanti. However, losing Mystery was more emotional than losing both of them. I knew that Aunt Hattie was older and she would not be around forever, but I expected that Mystery would be around indefinitely, and that we would have time to grow old together, as mother and daughter.

My job played a significant role in helping me get through during this difficult season. My talk show was called *Straight Talk*, which ended up being a very welcomed distraction. I was so busy, I did not have time to mourn day-in and day-out. The show was a Christian-based talk show where people called in for advice on a variety of subject matters. Most days, people were complaining about fighting at church, cheating ministers and deacons, outing pastors for their homosexuality etc.

One day, a lady called about reclaiming her family that she had abandoned a while ago because she was not properly prepared to be a wife or mother. She wanted specific advice from me about the best way to reclaim her family.

We chatted for a while and she said that she had been watching them from afar for the last year. She did not want to disrupt their lives, but wanted them to know that she still loved them. She said that she required assistance to be able to be a good wife and mother. Now that she had received the help that she needed, she was ready to fulfill her role in that capacity.

I asked her about her relationship with God and she informed me that she previously tried having a relationship with God; but she found out that all she needed to do was believe in herself. She is the one that got her the help she needed, not God.

I had a flashback to my teenage years when I thought there was no God, and that all I needed was myself in order to get by. I empathized with the caller's position, and relied on what I had learned in some of my classes to attempt to persuade her otherwise. The caller became irate and cussed me out, then disconnected from the call.

I felt defeated, as this was my first opportunity to attempt to help someone that I could relate with, but I obviously frustrated her. I thought back to the days that Aunt Hattie attempted to convince me that God was real, and how I mocked her and God. I tried to imagine what I could have said to the caller that would have made a difference in her life.

Four days later, the caller called back. I wanted to make certain that I did not lose her this time. When I recognized her voice, I motioned to the producer that this was the caller that I needed him to record the name and number in case she disconnected again. Although it was against the rules to contact callers, I thought that I could help her work through her spirituality. After all, she sounded like a good person that was ready to make amends for the pain that she may have caused in the past.

This time, she shared that she saw her husband and their child with some other folks and they all seemed to be happy. She told me that it appeared that her husband was dating a lady that had a daughter close to her son's age. She said she did not want to disrupt anything, but she deserved to have her family back. She never stopped loving them and wanted them to at least know that.

I attempted to direct the conversation back to her spirituality and the belief that there is a higher being that could be her support system while she faced this dilemma. She insisted that God never did her any favors, and he would not start now. She then said, "If you keep bringing up God, I will hang up on you again."

I responded by saying, "I am here to discuss whatever you want to discuss. After all, the show is called Straight Talk."

"Can you help me without bringing God's name into it?"

"That is difficult for me to do because God comes first and foremost in my life. I allow Him to direct my steps. So what I would do is pray for guidance from Him as to what the best thing for me to do. I must admit that God sometimes does not answer my prayers fast enough for me. So sometimes, I take things into my own hands. And that is when I mess up everything. So I have learned to be patient and listen for His guidance. It took me a while to really hear what God was saying. But after much practice, I have tuned my heart to His voice, and I hear Him loud and clear most of the time."

"Can you just try to not bring up God in our conversation, and tell me what you would do?" she asked.

"Well, if you are forcing me into my mortal self and away from my spiritual self, I would probably call my husband to let him know that I was alive and wanted to see him and my son."

"So, what if he says he wants nothing to do with me."

"I would pray for ..."

"No! No prayer! What would your mortal self do?"

IF LOVING ME IS WRONG

"I would tell him that I'm sorry for everything that I have done, or not done, over the past however many years, and ask him if he could find it in his heart to forgive me. With that, I would hope that we could start working toward some type of relationship."

"So, what if that did not work, what would you do?"

"Well, if he still did not come around, I probably would seek out the court system to enforce my rights to see my child."

"What if the problem is not with him? It is with the woman that he thinks he loves!"

"The woman that he loves has nothing to do with the relationship that you want with your child. Or does she?"

"I want my family back. I think I will just kill the bitch! Now that's straight talk!" *Click!*

The phone went silent. I said, "Hello, are you still there?"

The producer then went to a commercial. I got up and said, "What should we do? You have her number and name. Perhaps, we should call the police."

Jerry, the producer, said, "Oh, she probably is just venting. Relax. Take a break and we will start with the next caller."

I made it through the show but was somewhat shaken. I pryaed that the caller was not going to do anything rash. I sincerely hoped that she was just venting. I thought that maybe I should have stayed within my spiritual being, instead of my mortal being, as she requested. Perhaps I could have guided her toward

81

the right direction. If the caller called me again, I would ask God to direct my words to her. It was obvious that she was hurting, and by her last comment, she may also be disturbed.

I left work thinking about the caller and wishing that I had done things differently. I was supposed to meet Demetrius for dinner, but called him and told him that I had a difficult day and was going to call it a night. I thought about going over to Sweezy's to check on them, but was exhausted so I just went back to my place. When I arrived, Auntie Char was headed out the door for what looked like a date. I was happy for her, since I had not seen her date anyone in a long time.

She left smiling and said, "Don't wait up for me."

"You betta be good, Auntie!"

Auntie Char laughed and said, "I have been good for too long. It's time for me to be a little naughty."

I walked in and closed the door behind me, and thought about a nice relaxing bubble bath with a glass of merlot. I put down my stuff, and went into the bathroom to run some hot bath water with foaming bubbles, and bath beads. I then went to the kitchen to get some wine and I heard Auntie Char coming back in so I jokingly said, "What, did you forget your protection?"

There was no answer so I said, "Auntie Char!"

Still no answer, but I knew I heard the door. I walked into the living room, which was dark, and there was a strange figure standing there that looked like a woman holding a knife. I went into a calm mode and said, "Hi, can I help you?"

"Yes, I came to reclaim mines."

"I am sorry, reclaim yours?"

"Yes, that is what I said, Bitch."

When she said bitch, I realized that it was the voice from the caller earlier.

I remained calm and said, "Well, how can I help you with that?"

"By being a dead bitch!"

At that time it clicked. Everything came together. The family she had lost. Seeing her family with another woman. She must have been Demetrius ex-wife, Jordan. So I said, "Jordan?"

"Yes, it's me, Bitch."

"Jordan, this is not the right way to do it. Let's sit and talk together and collaborate on the best way to approach Demetrius."

"I don't need your help. I need you dead, Bitch!" And then she lunged at me with the knife. She tripped as she came forward; I then jumped on top of her, and wrestled with her to get the knife out of her hand. I cut myself on the blade, but I did not stop attempting to take the knife away. She rolled over and got on top of me. I screamed out, "God, help me!"

I don't know what happened, but the knife went flying across the floor and I got up and ran for the knife. She came running behind me screaming, "Bitch, I'm gonna kill you!" The next thing I heard was a knock on the door. I screamed at the top of my lungs, "Help! Help!"

Suddenly, a person burst through the door like superman. I made out the figure and could tell it was Poo Man, all five foot of him.

I shouted, "Call the police, Poo Man!"

Jordan got up from on top of me and bolted out the door, knocking Poo Man and his phone to the floor.

"What the hell was that?" asked Poo Man while running to help me up.

Once up, I hugged him and said, "Thank you, you just saved my life. Quick, give me your phone. I need to call the police. She may injure herself or someone else."

Poo man looked at my hand and said, "You're bleeding. You need help!"

I ignored him, and the blood, and called the police and explained to dispatch what happened. The dispatcher said she would call the report in, but in the meantime, make certain the premise was secure, and that an officer would be out immediately. After getting off the phone with the dispatcher, I immediately called Demetrius so he could be on alert; however, his phone went to voicemail. I screamed into the phone, "Demetrius, Jordan just tried to kill me and she may be going after you next!"

Chapter 13

Demetrius eventually got my message and came over to the house. When the police caught up with Jordan she was hiding in a ditch near my house. When I shared the news with Demetrius, he told me he wanted to go see her at the police station. I asked him whether he wanted me to go with him and he said, "No, I think it is best if I go alone." I wished him good luck and asked him to call me when he returned home.

I did not hear from Demetrius until the next day. He told me that he posted bail for Jordan because he did not believe she belonged in jail. I told him I agreed that she probably needed to be somewhere she could get professional counseling. He told me he had taken her to his house until they figured things out. I asked him had she met Colin, and he said that she had and they were bonding quite well. I don't know what made me ask the next question, but I asked, "Where did she sleep?"

"Porchia, why would you ask that question? Of course she slept in the guest room," he responded.

"Well, did she say how she found me?"

"No. We did not talk about that, but it is not difficult to track a celebrity like yourself down."

"Well, in one of the calls she said that the new girlfriend had a daughter."

"She probably saw you and Penny come over and assumed that she was your daughter."

"Oh, that makes sense. Hopefully you will get her the help she needs. I'm glad she has gotten the chance to see her son. Twelve years is a long time."

"It is. For both of them. Well, there are some things I am going to have to figure out. So I will be in touch later."

"Okay. I will be praying for you all."

"Thanks, we need it."

I hung up and said a prayer for them right away. I was not certain why it took Jordan twelve years for her to decide she wanted to see her son, but I am sure she had her reasons. I hoped that Demetrius would be able to get her the help that she needs to have a healthy relationship with her son. I was about to leave for the station when my phone rang. It was the Houston Police Department asking me whether I wanted to press charges against Jordan. I told them that it was all a misunderstanding, and that I did not want to press any charges.

My workday was much less stressful without calls from someone threatening to kill me. I called Tracy and asked her if she was interested in grabbing a bite to eat with me. She told me that she would be happy to join me and asked where would we meet. I told her I would pick her up so we could ride together. When I picked up Tracy, she was dressed as if we were going out on a night on the town. She told me that she wanted to go to the hottest dinner spot in Houston.

According to Tracy, the restaurant was a dinner jazz club where a lot of Houston's richest and finest men hung. She thought it would be a place where we could be truly entertained by potential suitors. It was a Friday night, and I was down for some entertainment after my difficult workweek. Actually, I had been under a lot of stress for the last six months. Although I was in my business attire, I felt comfortable enough to entertain Tracy and her wild idea.

We pulled up and the place seemed packed. There were no parking spaces anywhere. Luckily, there was valet parking, so I pulled up to let the attendant valet park the car. The attendant started flirting with Tracy and me. Of course she entertained him, so the guy thought he had a play at her, so he slipped his number to her. As he drove my car away, she tore up the paper, laughed, and said, "He could not even take me shopping at JC Penny on his minimum-wage job and tips."

"Trace, you are so vain! Come on let's go see what's happening in this place."

We rode the elevator to the thirty-fifth floor. We walked in and the host asked us if we had reservations. Tracy and I looked at each other then back at the Hostess and said, "No," in unison.

Tracy then asked, "Do we need a reservation? There are only two of us."

"Yes, reservations are recommended. As you see, the restaurant gets rather crowded on Friday nights."

Tracy, being her snooty self said, "Will you, or will you not be able to sit us within the next five minutes?"

"I probably will have a table available for you in about thirty minutes," responded the hostess back in a voice similar to Tracy's.

I wanted to laugh but knew not to instigate the situation because Tracy would go to the left.

Tracy then said, "Is Ronald here?"

The hostess' attitude changed and she asked, "Oh, do you know Ronald?"

"Yes, he is my uncle. And I am certain if I told him that I was informed by you that I had to wait on a table for thirty minutes, he would not find that acceptable!"

The hostess said, "Miss."

"Yes, Ms. Charles," said Tracy.

"Ms. Charles, let me check to see if I can find a table for two. Give me a moment. I will be right back."

I looked at Tracy and asked, "Which one of your uncles own this dinner club?"

"Girl, Uncle Rick's man owns this club."

"Your uncle Rick is gay?"

"He is 55, has never been married, and has no kids. You do the math."

"That does not mean that he is gay!"

"Have you ever seen him with a woman?"

"No, but..."

"No but nothing. He put the "g" in gay, girl. Get over it!" Tracy snapped her fingers and waved her hand from side to side downwardly making a "Z."

As I was about to say something to Tracy when the hostess returned and said, "I found a table for two with a beautiful view overlooking the city. You can't see the band, but you will still hear them."

"No problem. I am sure my uncle appreciates your effort to find something for us. What is your name so I can put in a good word for you?"

"My name is Diamani."

"Well, thank you, Diamani. You've been quite helpful," said Tracy in her snooty voice again.

A handsome young man came and led us to our table. Of course, Tracy started flirting with him.

We sat at a corner table that had a spectacular view of the City. I looked at Tracy and said, "Girl, you worked your magic or demon, whichever you prefer to say."

"Look I got us a seat, didn't I?. You need to learn to be more appreciative of my talents."

"What talent is that, being a bitch?"

"Oh, no Ms. Mighty and Saved Porchia did not just use the B word."

"I am going to need a stiff drink dealing with you tonight. Can you work your magic and get me a drink right away?" I asked.

A short waiter who resembled Spike Lee came over as if he heard our conversation. I told him to make me a dirty martini, shaken, not stirred.

"Bring me something tall, dark and strong, like I like my men," said Tracy while looking the little short man up and down with her nose turnt up.

"Ma'am, I will certainly bring you back a 'Fuck You Too'," the waiter said without missing a beat.

When he walked away, I laughed and said, "I think I like him."

"Whateva, I wouldn't even let that little short muthafuka smell my pussy."

"Ouch, my ears!"

I glanced to the table to my left and I could have sworn I saw the back of a man that looked like Demetrius. I asked Tracy to look over to see if that was Demetrius. She said, "Girl it looks just like him. And some woman just joined him at the table."

I looked over and it was Demetrius and Jordan. I had a direct view of Jordan who was on point in a short red beaded cocktail dress. Her body was exquisitely attached to every thread of her dress. I then saw Demetrius reach over and hold her hand as he was talking to her. I did not know whether to go to their table, run out of the restaurant, or stay and pretend that I did not see them. I know all of the color must have disappeared from my face. Tracy made the decision for me and said, "Come on Sister. Let's go!"

I followed Tracy out of the restaurant using the opposite aisle where Demetrius and Jordan were sitting, hoping that they did not see us. The waiter was on the way to the table with our drinks, so I grabbed the martini and gulped it down. I looked at him and said, "It's on her uncle," and kept walking.

I was so humiliated. I could not believe that Demetrius would play me and not be upfront that he wanted to get back with his ex-wife. Had he really gotten a divorce as he told me?

Once the valet returned with my car, Tracy told me that she would drive. We drove around the city for a while. She asked me if I was hungry and I told her that I had lost my appetite. She asked me whether I wanted to talk about what happened, and I told her no. So we just drove for hours around the Loop until she suggested that we go to the Coushatta Casino. I looked at her and said, "No I don't feel like riding there. Let's catch a plane to Vegas."

"Vegas? I don't have money to just get up and go to Vegas like that?"

"I do. Let's go."

"I don't have any clothes for Vegas."

"We'll shop when we get there. Come on, live a little."

"Okay, what the hell. If you're game, I'm game."

I called Sweezy; then Auntie Char to let them know I would be gone for the weekend. Sweezy wanted to play twenty questions, so I told him I would talk to him when

I returned. He told me to be careful and that he loved me.

Chapter 14

It was early in the morning when we arrived in Vegas. I was tired and had not slept in over twenty-four hours. When I turned on my phone, I noticed I had several missed calls from Demetrius, but he had not left any messages. I wondered whether he saw me at the restaurant. I was checking into the Bellagio when my phone rang. It was Demetrius again.

I decided to let his call go to voicemail because this was not an appropriate time to speak with him. Plus, I did not know what I was going to say. I thought Demetrius and I were headed toward a trusting, loving, and lasting relationship. What I saw turned my world upside down. Not the upside down that happened when I caught Ty in bed with Raheem, but an upside down where my world was completely shaken. How could Demetrius betray the trust I had bestowed upon him?

I told Tracy I needed to crash for a bit before hitting the town. Tracy had never been to Vegas, so she went out to see what was going on out on the Strip. The minute I started drifting asleep my phone rang. I did not know if I had enough energy to speak with Demetrius, but I did not want to put him off any longer. I answered the phone, "Hello."

"Hey, Pocahontas. How are you?"

"Ty?"

"Yes, who else would be calling you saying, 'Hey Pocahontas'?"

I responded, "Penny."

He laughed and said, "I'm sure I don't sound like Penny."

"I'm sorry, I was just resting. And the phone caught me off guard."

"Would you like for me to let you rest."

"No, not really."

"Well, what's wrong?"

"Nothing. I guess congratulations is in order. I read you were getting married."

"Getting married?"

"Yeah, it was announced on *True Entertainment*."

"I am not certain what was announced, but I am not marrying anyone."

"Oh, guess you can't believe everything you hear."

"Pocahontas, you should know that by now."

"Well, I can't even believe everything I see."

"What are you talking about?"

"Oh, nothing. So how have you been?"

"Okay. Thanks for checking on Penny when she was in Houston. All she does is talk about you."

"You know she is always a joy to be around."

"I'm in Houston. I would like to take you out tomorrow to thank you. Would that be possible?"

"I'm in Vegas."

"Vegas! What are you doing in Vegas?"

"I just needed to get away for a minute. Life has been rough lately."

"Yeah, I heard about Mystery. I am so sorry. I wanted to come to her service, but I could not get away. Then Poo Man told me about some crazy incident at your house with a fan from the radio show or something."

"Yeah or something."

"So where are you staying?"

"We are at Bellagio."

"We?"

"Yes, Trace and I."

"Oh, okay, well, you two be careful. Hopefully I will see you soon."

"Okay, take care."

Ty took my mind off of Demetrius temporarily. But I knew that I could not just keep avoiding Demetrius' calls. I picked up my cell to call him, and Tracy came back into the room and said, "I absolutely love this place! I would not mind moving here."

"Trace, you're just enchanted. You would not want to live here. You would be a long way from Houston."

"No, I think I could live here!"

"What would you do?"

"I don't know. Work in the casino."

"Doing what?"

"A barmaid, dancer, something, I don't know."

"You wouldn't know rhythm if it hit you in the face."

"Thanks for having so much confidence in me, Sister Dearest."

I laughed because it reminded of Mystery and the name I called her.

"So, are you ready to go shopping?" I asked.

"Yes, on your dime. I am ready for anything."

We left the hotel to go find some clothes. I ended up spending over three thousand dollars on clothes, shoes, and accessories for Tracy and me. Then we went to lunch at a Moroccan restaurant. It was the first time Tracy had eaten Moroccan food. She was like a kid when we walked in and had to sit on the floor. She became really excited when she found out that we ate with our fingers instead of utensils. The belly dancer was definitely over the top for her. She took so many pictures on her camera phone, you would think she had a thing for women. It was great being in her presence, because she made me temporarily forget about the heartache I left back in Houston.

When we returned to the hotel with our new clothing, I was anxious to take a shower and change into fresh clothes. I could hear the hotel phone ring from the shower. I heard Tracy carrying on a conversation with someone and I assumed it was a person she met while she went out on her discovery trip on the Strip. When I walked into the room Tracy was staring at me with a smile on her face.

"What is wrong with you?" I asked.

"So, you just had to tell your man that we were here so he could join you."

"Demetrius is here?"

"I am not talking about Demetrius. That was Ty."

"Ty?"

"Yes, Ty!"

"He asked for you to give him a call." "Where is he staying?" I asked.

"Here, in the Presidential Suite, of course."

"Really?"

"Yes, really!" Tracy said batting her eyes.

My phone rang and Tracy looked and said, "That is probably him again."

I ran to the phone and said, "Hello."

"Where are you, Porchia? I have been everywhere looking for you."

"Well, if you would have looked yesterday, I was not far away."

"What are you talking about?"

"Nothing."

"So, where are you?"

"I'm in Vegas."

"What are you doing in Vegas?"

"Allowing you time to get everything together there."

"What?"

"Look, Demetrius, I saw you at dinner last night with your wife. And you looked rather chummy together."

"You were at *Moving on Up*?"

"Yes, I was there. I saw it all."

"Porchia, I decided to take Jordan out to talk about getting her help."

"Well, looked like you were enjoying her company in that little sexy red dress she was wearing."

"I can't control what she wears."

"But you can control holding her hand, looking into her eyes, whispering sweet nothings."

"Porchia, I don't know what you think you saw, but it was not what you are portraying."

"So, my eyes are lying, Demetrius?"

"I don't know what is going on, but I can tell you that it was nothing romantic going on between us last night. We were talking about getting her counseling, finding her housing, and working out a co-parenting plan when she thinks she's ready."

"We can talk more about this when I get back," I said.

"Is this the way you handle problems, by running away?"

I paused before answering him. Aunt Hattie told me once that I could not keep running away from everything. Hesitantly I answered, "Perhaps."

"Well, please don't run from me. Let's talk about it, and work it out."

When I ended the call with Demetrius, Tracy said, "Whoa, what did he say?"

"I don't want to talk about it now. Go take a shower so we can go out on the town."

Tracy went to take a shower and I decided to call Ty. When he answered, I asked him why was he stalking me.

"It sounded as if you needed a friend."

"I told you I was with Tracy."

"As I said, sounded like you needed a friend."

I laughed and said, "Ty, don't talk about my family like that."

"Don't front! You know Tracy better than I do."

"Yes, I do. And I probably know you better than you know yourself. So what are you really doing here?"

"I just wanted to make certain you were okay. Especially after speaking with Poo Man about your stalker."

I mumbled under my breath, "You are the only stalker I know."

"Sorry, I did not understand what you said."

"You have no responsibility for me, Ty."

"Yeah, but I still have love for you."

"So is that why you were all hugged up with Angie Stone?"

"Ha! You are funny. She is just a good friend."

"A good friend with benefits?" I asked.

"I am not asking you about your sex life, why are you digging into mine?"

"So you are sleeping with her."

"Porchia, why are you attacking me? What's up with you, I only came to make sure you were okay."

"Men!"

"Let's call it a truce. Can we meet up for drinks, coffee, dinner or something?"

"The or something sounds good to me," I responded.

"Pocahontas?"

"Ty?"

"I will see you soon," he said, before ending the call.

Tracy came out of the shower and there was a knock on my door. I looked at Tracy and said, "You may want to grab your clothes and dress in the bathroom, that's Ty."

"I think I want to dress in front of Ty."

I looked at her and walked toward the door and said, "Suit yourself."

From the side of my eyes, I saw Tracy running into the bathroom with her clothes.

When I opened the door, Ty was standing there in an off white linen suit, showing his pearly white teeth and dimples. I looked at him and said, "Well, hello there, Mr. Suave."

"Oh, how did I earn that title?"

"Guess you were born that way."

Tracy came bouncing out the bathroom looking at Ty saying, "Oh, you look finger licking good, Mr. Gamble."

"Well, what have you been doing Tracy? You are looking more and more Hollywood yourself."

"You two seem like you are each other's biggest fans." I said.

Tracy flirtatiously said, "No, I am certain Mr. Gamble has many, many fans."

Ty laughed and looked at Tracy and said, "I hope you don't mind me stealing your sister for a minute."

"No, you two kids have fun. I don't mind finding my own fun. I'm loving Vegas."

Ty winked at Tracy and said, "Yeah, and I bet Vegas is loving you too."

They were really making me sick with all of their adorning talk so I said, "Well, since you two have made plans for me, Ty, you better take me now or never."

"Pocahontas, I could not live with never, so let's go now. See you later, Tracy," Ty said as he walked toward me, grabbed my hand, and opened the door.

I looked back at Tracy and winked at her as Ty and I walked out of the door.

Tracy mouthed, "You Jezebel."

I mouthed back to her, "You are just jealous." She flipped me off before I closed the door.

Chapter 15

Ty had a driver waiting for us once we exited the hotel. I asked him what were we doing and he told me to be patient. We drove about thirty minutes to the desert where we had all-terrain vehicles waiting for us. I looked at him and said, "Ty, I am not getting on that."

"What, you afraid of getting a lil' dirty?"

"No, but you are the one in a white linen suit!"

"There are plenty more where this came from," he said while taking off his jacket.

He pushed me out of the car and next thing I knew Ty was strapping my helmet on, and this guy started showing me how to operate the ATV. I looked at Ty and asked, "Why can't I just ride with you?"

"You would not want to do that, Pocahontas."

We started riding and the first thing that Ty did was a donut, making dust fly everywhere. I was glad I was on my own vehicle. He waved his arms as to say come on and he sped off. I started my vehicle and was a little intimidated at first, but after Ty edged me on, I gunned the vehicle and felt an exhilaration that I had not felt in a long time. We were hitting sand dunes and bouncing high in the desert. We rode for about an hour then turned and made our way back to our car. By the time I got off the ATV, I was excited about doing something I had never done before. Ty looked at me and said, "Now you're ready for our real adventure."

I looked at him and his outfit had turned from offwhite to gray. I smiled and said, "No, Ty, that is about as adventurous as I will get in one day."

"So you think!"

We drove about twenty minutes up this mountain and when the car stopped, I could see people zip lining across the canyon. My mouth opened wide, and my eyes opened even wider. Ty could not stop laughing and I just shook my head from side-to-side. Ty said, "C'mon, Pocahontas, this will be fun."

"Have you ever done this before? It does not look safe!" I screamed.

"I have not, but I researched the company and there has never been an accident."

"I don't want to be the first!"

"That is irrational, Pocahontas. You have as much of a chance of being injured as you have a chance of being struck by lightning."

"Living in Houston, that probability is high!"

Ty finally talked me into getting out of the car, but I told him I had to watch other people go before I did it. Four people at a time would go so I stood there until about twelve people left. Ty looked at me and said, "Okay, are you ready?"

"No I am not, but let's get this over with!"

We listened to a fifteen-minute safety instruction, which I was uncertain of what was being said because my heart was beating so fast and loud, I thought everyone around me heard it. The next thing I noticed was the attendant strapping me into this contraption and all I could do was pray and ask God to watch over me. Ty was next to me smiling and waving like a buffoon. I could not believe I let him talk me into this. I asked the attendant once it starts, how does it stop? He told me that it would stop when I was at the end of the ride. That really concerned me because the one thing I wanted to do was skydive, but I was always concerned about what would happen if the chute did not open.

I closed my eyes and just stepped out on faith and I started slowly going down the slope. I decided to open my eyes and saw the beautiful canyon below me. Within minutes, I was moving at about fifty mph on the cable. I looked over to see if I could see Ty and he was in front of me flailing his arms and legs. I was feeling an adrenaline rush like I had never felt before. I wish I could have bottled the feeling. In addition, the view was remarkable. I could see all sorts of colors such as rust, brown, and orange flashing before my eyes. It would have been spectacular to videotape the ground below me.

I was admiring the beautiful landscape when the ride slowed down and I could see the other side. Ty was already being unharnessed as I was approaching the landing spot. I wish there was a way that I could have stopped the ride and just admired the beauty below me.

By the time I reached the other side, I knew that I was all-smiles.

Ty looked at me. "Felt liberating, didn't it?"

As I thought about it, it was a type of freedom that I hadn't felt before. I impulsively hugged him and said, "Thank you so much Ty."

As we got into the car, Ty looked at me and said, "You are so beautiful."

I blushed and said, "What has gotten into you?"

"You have gotten into me and will never leave me. Now tell me what's wrong?"

"Nothing's wrong. I had a wonderful, adventurous day."

"No, I am here because when we were on the phone I could tell something was wrong with you."

"I don't want to think about that now. I am feeling too good right now. Let's not spoil the moment."

"Okay, fair enough. But is there anything I can do to help?"

"You already have," I said while putting my head on his shoulder.

Ty put his arms around me. "I wish I could do so much more."

We arrived back at the hotel and Ty asked me if I would join him for dinner. I did not want anything to go further than it had already, so I told him that I needed to spend time with Tracy, but I appreciated everything that he had done to make my day a memorable one. He asked me whether he could at least walk me back to my room.

I told him that it was best to say our goodbyes in the lobby.

"Okay, Pocahontas. But remember, I am here..."

"Yes, if I need you. I know Ty, and I appreciate that."

He leaned down and kissed me on my forehead. I smiled and walked to the elevator. I wanted so badly to look back at him, but I knew if I did, he would see the tears in my eyes.

When I arrived back in the room there was no Tracy. I thought about soaking in the Jacuzzi bathtub, but remembered I needed to wash my hair, so opted for a shower instead. I thought about the day's events and how wonderful it was to spend time with Ty again.

Then my thoughts drifted back to Demetrius. I could hear Aunt Hattie saying, "Baby, you can't keep running." I knew at that time I would have to directly deal with Demetrius and his estranged wife.

After taking my shower, I laid on the bed and drifted off to sleep. When I woke up it was two a.m. and still there was no Tracy. I became worried so I called her phone. When she answered the phone, I could hear loud music in the background. She said, "Hey, Sister. What are you doing? You should come join the party I am at." "I was just calling because I was worried about you. You know our plane leaves in about five hours, right?"

"Yeah, Javier will just drop me off at the airport. I will see you there."

"Trace, who is Javier?"

"The man I will marry. Okay, girl. Gotta go. See you soon."

I just stared at my phone. When will Tracy get a clue? I decided that I needed to increase my prayers for her from daily to hourly!

Chapter 16

Tracy was the last one to board the plane. They closed the doors shortly after she boarded, so I imagined that she almost missed the plane. She arrived looking disheveled in her party clothes, smelling like alcohol and sex. I looked at her and rolled my eyes.

"Oh, get your panties out of your butt. Just because you live like a nun, that does not mean I have to!"

I started to snap and tell her that she also did not have to live like a tramp, but decided not to cause a ruckus on the plane. I said, "Do you!"

Then I laid my head back on my seat, and closed my eyes so she would not say another word. I could imagine her pouting because I knew that she wanted to tell me all about Javier, but I did not have the energy to listen to her excitement about something that was a one-night fling.

When we landed she said, "Are you going to talk to me now?"

"I don't have anything to say, Trace. You never listen anyway."

"No, this is real this time. I really like Javier, and he likes me more than I like him. I am going back next weekend to see him."

"Why are you running to him?"

"Well, he is paying for it."

"Never mind, Trace. You don't get it."

I was happy when the pilot put the seatbelt sign off and the ding went off to allow us to get off the plane. I walked fast as Tracy tried to keep up with me in her eight inch heels. When we got to the car she said, "Porchia, you are being ridiculous."

"And you are still acting like a ho. Did counseling not help you get over what your father did to you?"

I immediately regretted what I said when the words came out of my mouth. Tears began welling up in Tracy's eyes.

"Sorry, Trace. I did not mean it."

Tracy did not respond.

I dropped her off at her apartment and told her bye and that I appreciated her going to Vegas with me. She did not even look at me as she got out of the car. She shut the door and walked up the sidewalk. I sat there looking at her knowing that I was out of line bringing up what our child molesting father did to her. I prayed silently for her to forgive my mean-spirited comments. I only wanted the best for her, and was not certain how to communicate it in a positive fashion when she repeatedly did things that were counterproductive to having a healthy relationship.

After dropping Tracy off, I decided that I wanted to deal with Demetrius right away. I drove to his house and called him to tell him I was pulling up in his driveway. He hesitated and said, "Uh okay." He met me at the door and said, "This is really not a good time."

"What do you mean this is not a good time?"

"Jordan just had a minor breakdown that I am trying to deal with."

"Why is she still here?"

"I have not found a place for her yet."

I could see Jordan walking toward the door. She asked, "Baby, who is at the door?"

As she walked closer, I could see that she was wearing a negligee and a robe loosely tied around her waist. She looked at me and said, "Oh, Porchia, so nice of you to come by. Honey, you are being so rude. Porchia, I have cooked a marvelous breakfast. Would you like to come in and join me and my family for breakfast?"

I looked at Demetrius, and he hung his head down.

I responded, "No, thank you. Enjoy your family," and walked away.

Within minutes of pulling away, Demetrius called me and I let it go to voicemail. I picked up the voicemail and he left a message saying, "I am so sorry, Porchia. Jordan is delusional. She thinks that we are a family, and I am having a difficult time letting her know that what we had is over. I love you and want you I just need to deal with this issue first. I will be in touch soon."

I responded to his voicemail and said, "Demetrius, please don't bother to contact me again. I wish you and Jordan much success in life. It was a pleasure reacquainting with you. Perhaps at another time, and in another place. God bless you."

Lord, are you telling me that is your desire that I be alone? I want to please you Lord, but I don't want to spend the next fifty plus years without a mate. But if it is your will, let your will be done. I know that I can do anything with you as my Guide. I just need to know.

I needed something to make me smile because I felt like I was slowly dying on the inside. I drove to Sweezy's to see Sly. They were not there when I arrived. Ms. Marvelle told me that they had gone to church. I thought that, perhaps, I could meet them at church. Sweezy attended Sadiq's church; therefore, I was hesitant to go to the church. Although the church was large; I did not want Sadiq to feel uncomfortable if he happened to see me.

When I looked at the time, I realized that church service was almost over so I texted Sweezy and asked him if he wanted to join me for brunch. He texted back that he would love to and sent me the address where he wanted to meet up.

I arrived and was waiting for Sweezy and Sly to arrive when I heard a voice say, "Teepee! Teepee! I missed you!"

I picked up a smiling Sly and told him, "I missed you more!"

Sweezy came and kissed me on my cheek, "Are you okay?"

I smiled. "No, I am not okay. But I am doing much better now that I am with my two most favorite guys in the whole wide world," while kissing Sly repeatedly on his cheeks.

He laughed and said, "Teepee, you are slobbering on me."

I put him down and said, "Okay, one day you will miss my slobbering mister."

Once we were seated, I told Sweezy that I was starving and that I would take Sly to the buffet so we could get something to eat. Spending time with Sly took my mind away from all of my troubles. He made me smile and laugh throughout brunch.

I had a temporary moment of sadness thinking how great it would be for Mystery to be here smiling and laughing with us. I caught Sweezy several times drifting into his own world. I knew that I had to get some alone time with him to find out how he was really doing. He had sold all of the clubs, with the exception of Aunt Hattie's Retreat, to spend more time with Sly.

When he was gazing into the atmosphere I said, "What's up, Pops?"

He laughed and said, "Swoosh, you got problems."

"So what have you been up to, Pappa Sweezy?"

"Just trying to settle on all of the transactions I have made over the last month. I am going to need to find a good accountant and lawyer."

"Oh, it must be difficult having so much money!"

"Swoosh, if you only knew."

"Any time you want to get rid of any, I am here."

"You may get what you ask for. Who said, mo' money, mo' problems? But I know you're pulling it in with your books and your radio show. I hear people saying they listen to you all the time."

"You know that is funny. I never thought that so many people would listen to a radio talk show."

"Did you see that your friend landed on a sitcom?"

"Who?"

"Mookie."

"Really? No, I did not. I have not spoken with him recently. But I will have to call him."

"Yeah, he has a leading role. I watched it, and it was pretty funny."

"Cool!"

"So other than your too much money issues, how are things?"

"Just trying to be here for my little man. Sly, did you tell Teepee that you are playing peewee football?"

"No and Teepee, daddy is my coach!" screamed Sly.

"He is?"

"Yes, we have a lot of fun at practice. We are called the Mysterees."

I looked up at Sweezy and he just smiled.

"Leave it to your daddy. He will buy you a professional team next and call them the Queens," I said laughing.

"Humn, I like that idea," laughed Sweezy.

We sat until most of the brunch crowd was gone. I told Sweezy that I should get home to Auntie Char, since I had not spoken with her since I left town. Sweezy looked at me and said, "Yeah, we need to talk about why you left H-Town like the feds was on your tail."

"We will, Pops!"

I kissed them both and headed toward home. I decided to try to reach Mookie and he answered right away and said, "She lives!"

"What's up, Mook?"

"God is good, Ms. Lady. I have been blessed immensely. But I miss you."

"Oh, yeah? I guess that is why I have not heard from you."

"My schedule has been crazed! But I was going to call you because I need your address."

"Are you coming to visit me?" I asked.

"I wish I could get away. But no, I need to send you an invite."

"An invite to what?"

"An invite to my wedding."

"What! Are you marrying Rechelle?"

"That hoochie. Hell naw! I am marrying Nitra Thomas."

"Professor Nitra Thomas!"

"Yep! The one and only."

"What? Isn't she like fifty years old?"

"What do da cougars say these days? Fifty is the new thirty. She is everything I ever wanted in a woman. And I mean evraythang!"

I laughed and said, "Please, spare me the details."

"Yeah, I know your virgin ears can't handle that."

"Straight talk. Okay, I will text you my address when I get home."

"Cool. So how are you and the good Doctor doing these days?"

"It's old and over."

"What?"

"Yep. His psycho, estranged, drug addict wife, who left him and his son twelve years ago, attacked me in my home with a machete. After the attack, he decided he would move her back into his home."

"Damn, Ms. Lady, that sounds like a movie!"

"Yep a love tragedy, starring your popular love-struck actress Porchia Williams. You know I think I am going to change my name. Perhaps Porchia DuBois will have better luck than Porchia Williams."

"Hey, one day love will find you."

"I hope I am not too old to see it."

"You won't be Ms. Lady. You are a hell of a catch!"

"Yeah, according to who?"

"I am the authority on catches. And one day you will be as happy as I am with Nitra. I would love to talk more, but I have to run. I love you."

"And I you. We'll talk soon."

"Until, Ms. Lady."

Chapter 17

The following morning I called an attorney to initiate my name change from Porchia Williams to Porchia Williams DuBois. Porchia Williams DuBois, a new woman with a new perspective, and the proud daughter of Mystery DuBois. I announced it on my show that *Straight Talk* was being hosted by Porchia Williams Dubois. I initially received a lot of calls asking whether I had gotten married.

I was supposed to be fielding calls, but I decided to dedicate my show to Mystery and her struggles of raising a daughter who was the result of a rape. I received more calls than the switchboard could handle. Some calls telling me that I should be proud of where I came from and the strength of my mother, others sharing their tales of abuse, incest, and molestation. The producer looked at me and said, "Porchia, you went off script but this was one of the most successful shows. Perhaps you should bring a topic each time and let the public react."

I was fine with his suggestion, because this was one of the most therapeutic shows I had ever done. It was great that we were in syndication, because I received calls from all over the United States, including Puerto Rico. Listening to women who have overcome some of the most difficult circumstances made me realize that there is hope for Tracy. I hoped that she listened to the show and felt encouragement from these women.

But even more important, I had a new-found respect for my mother. I am not certain whether she ever went to counseling for what happened to her, but she came out a hell of a woman. I knew that Aunt Hattie had a lot to do with it, but Mystery defeated the ghosts of her past to become an amazing person.

I visited my mother's grave to share my newfound admiration for her. I spilled out everything that I felt in the past, I apologized for how I treated her, and told her how proud I was to be her daughter. If only she was alive to hear me say the words, "Mother, from this day forth, I will honor you and your memory."

I pulled out my cell phone right there and asked Sweezy if we could meet. He told me that he could meet me at his house around seven that night. In the meantime, I called an attorney to share my idea with him.

I met with Sweezy and asked him how he would feel if we started several group homes in the Houston metropolitan area for sexually abused, pregnant teenagers. He thought it would be a great idea. I asked him whether he would invest in such a venture and he said, "Whatever you need Swoosh."

"I want to name it after Mystery. I am just having a hard time deciding what to call it."

"How about Mystery's Retreat?"

118

"Nah, that is too close to what we call Aunt Hattie's place."

At that time, Sly came into the room and I jokingly asked, "What would you call a place dedicated to the memory of your mother?"

He put his hand under his chin and went into what looked like a deep thought and then came out with, "Mommy's Heaven."

From that I said, "What about, 'Mommy's Haven'."

Sly said, "Is that like a heaven?"

I responded, "Yes, it's like heaven on earth for people who need help."

"I like it, Teepee!"

Sweezy looked and said, "Well, Mommy's Haven it is."

I found a renewed energy in investing my time in developing "Mommy's Haven" and managing my show. I did not realize I did not have a life or friends until I received Mookie's invite to his wedding in North Carolina and wanted someone to travel with me.

In the past, it would have been my sister, mother or aunt. Tracy picked up and moved to Vegas with Javier. She was busy helping him manage his real estate business, which was just one of many businesses that he owned. To my surprise, he ended up being a legit businessman that was actually crazy about Tracy. Both of them partied too much for my taste, but they seemed to be equally yoked.

Auntie Char was busy with her club and her new man as well. I rarely saw her at the house. Most of the time she spent with him at his place. I was still waiting to meet him, and she promised that I would soon. However, six months passed and I still had not met Ronnie. Although I asked Auntie Char why was she keeping her man away, it really did not matter whether I met him; all I knew was that he made Auntie Char extremely happy. When at home, she was always walking around singing and dancing with a big smile on her face.

I found a new church and had met a few females, but none of them were particularly friendly toward me; although I made every effort to engage them. There were also a couple of guys that flirted with me, but I always ignored their comments.

I was left to hanging out with Sweezy and Sly, and I did not think either of them would be an appropriate date for a wedding. As I was brainstorming who would I go with to North Carolina, he called.

"Well, hello, Mr. Gamble. What do I owe this call to?"

"Penny."

"Is everything okay?"

"Other than being expensive. Yeah, she is okay."

"So what's up?"

"Well, she wants to go to Paradise Islands in the Caribbean for her birthday. And she wants none other than a trip with you and me to Paradise Island."

I laughed and said, "What?"

"Yep, that was her request. I told her that I did not think you would be able to make it. I asked her if she be happy if it was just me and her. Her response was, 'I guess'. So I called you to see if you could join us as a surprise to her."

"Actually, that sounds like fun. When?" I asked.

"September thirteenth."

"Yeah, I can make that for quid pro quo." "Now you are talking Latin?" he laughed.

"I need a date to a wedding in two weeks. Can you attend with me?"

"I can. Any special attire?"

"Yeah, wear your clown suit."

"Okay, I will have to take it to the cleaners today," he snickered. "I am assuming the wedding is in Houston?"

"No, it is North Carolina."

"Well, I am going to do it right. I will fly to Houston so we can arrive in North Carolina together."

"Okay. Sounds good."

"I will come a little early to let Penny spend time with her grandmother. Then I will drop her off at Aunt Verdie's while I accompany you to the wedding."

"Sounds like a plan, Mr. Gamble."

"So where is this Mr. Gamble coming from?" Ty asked.

"I am just trying to keep you in the right frame of mind."

"Believe me, when it comes to you, I am always in the right frame of mind."

"You are a great friend, Ty."

"One day you will realize that I am more than a friend."

"Bye Ty!"

"See you soon, Pocahontas."

When I hung up with Ty, I realized that I needed to expand my social network. It was sad that the only date I could get for a wedding was my ex-boyfriend from high school.

Chapter 18

Sweezy and I had been working really hard on "Mommy's Haven" until the wee hours of the morning. Therefore, I spent most nights at his house. It also gave me a reason to be close to Sly and Ms. Marvelle, who made the best meals.

I decided to go home late one night to give Sweezy and Sly a break from my overbearing ways. It seemed like I was turning into Mystery and being overly protective when it came to both of them.

I walked into our house and Auntie Char's man, Ronnie, was on top of her, eating her out on our sofa. I thought, *Ugh, time for a new sofa.*

They both jumped up and Auntie Char said, "Oh, Porchia, I am sorry. I did not realize that you were coming home tonight."

To my surprise, it was not Ronnie, but a BBW, the name that women with extra weight refer to themselves as. She was a beautiful brown lady, with a lot junk in her trunk accompanied by extra storage in her belly, arms and legs.

I must have been staring in disbelief, because the woman pulled up her pants and broke the silence by saying, "Hi, Porchia. I'm Roni. I've heard a lot about you."

I blurted out, "Well, I obviously did not hear enough about you."

Auntie Char said, "Well, I am glad you two have finally met."

I looked at Auntie Char and was not quite sure how to respond. I said, "You two carry on, I'll just be in my room."

"No, Porchia, you don't have to go into your room. We should have been in my room. I apologize. I just really did not expect to see you tonight."

Roni said, "I am going to call it a night, baby. I will let you and Porchia spend time together. I know you have not seen each other in a while, and you probably have a lot to talk about."

I muttered under my breath, "That is an understatement."

Then Roni and Auntie Char started passionately kissing in front of me. I stood there in complete shock, not knowing whether to walk away, or just keep staring. Auntie Char said, "I love you, baby."

Roni responded, "I love you more, Bae. Lata, Porchia."

"Nice to finally meet you, Roni," I said.

When Roni left, I looked at Auntie Char and said, "Wow, I did not expect that."

"I am so sorry you found out this way, Porchia. I had been planning on talking to you about us."

"When, Char? When you walked down the aisle with Roni?"

"You know that women marrying each other in Texas, although legal, is still not universally accepted."

"That is beside the point. Did you not think you could share this with me?"

"No, do you realize what your face said when you saw Roni?"

"Yes, I was in shock because you pretended Roni was a man!"

"Did you see your face when we kissed each other?"

"No, but…"

"That look said it all. It was a look of disgust."

"No, in all fairness, it was still a look of shock."

"Okay, Porchia. Your aunt is a woman who is in love with another woman."

"So how long have you been a lesbian?"

"I don't like titles," Auntie Char responded.

"Okay, how long have you been a woman liking other women?'"

"After Mystery saved my life with the bone marrow."

"Did Mystery know?"

"Yes, she did."

"Does Sweezy know?"

"Anything that Mystery knew, you know Sweezy also knew."

"Dang, am I the only one in this family that did not know?"

"I did not think it was important. You knew that I was dating someone. What difference does it make if it is a woman or a man?"

"It makes a big difference, Auntie Char. I would have not been in shock when I found the two of you on the sofa. I thought we were close, and that you felt comfortable enough to share this type of information with me. I feel like you are treating me as I would have treated Mystery."

"Porchia, I am sorry. Sometimes you come off as condemning, instead of understanding. I know your doctrine probably states that women loving women is wrong. But I know it is right in my heart."

"Actually, you don't know what my views are about homosexuality. In theological school, I spent a lot of my time researching and soul searching."

"And what did you conclude about homosexuality."

"I concluded that God loves us all. And I have no right to judge. God is the ultimate judge."

"So what does that mean?"

"It means, I am okay with whatever choices you make, as it relates to your sexuality. The reasons for your choices are between you and God."

"So you are still not saying whether it's right or wrong."

"I am in no position to make that determination."

"Are you going to treat me differently?" Auntie Char asked.

"Auntie Char, I will always love you for who you are, not for what I think you should be, what I would like you to be, or who you love or don't love. But I may not walk around you naked anymore," I said laughing.

She hit me upside of my head and said, "Come here, girl. I love you."

We hugged and I said, "I love you too. But you owe us a new couch. Gross!"

"It's about time we update our furniture anyway. No telling what has been done on this couch before," said Auntie Char.

"Yeah, you are right about that. Especially with Mystery living here," I said.

"Well, I heard Aunt Hattie was a mess back in her day too. So I don't know," said Auntie Char.

We both laughed and I asked, "Are you hungry?"

Auntie Char responded, "Yeah, I was gonna get my eat on before you so rudely interrupted us."

"Ugh that was TMI, Auntie!"

We went into the kitchen and began cooking up a feast. It was after midnight and we were still laughing and talking at the kitchen table. This brought up old memories of Auntie Hattie and me at the kitchen table. I looked at our table and realized that it may be time for an update, but there was no way I could get rid of this "comfort table."

Chapter 19

Ty and I attended Mookie's star-studded wedding. For once, Ty was the least recognized person at the wedding. However, during this period in his career, Ty was a professional at dealing with his celebrity status. He was always polite to everyone he met. And if they were kids, he took extra time to spend with them. I must admit that Penny had brought out the best in him. He seemed to be kinder, patient, and more loving than I remembered. He attended to all of my needs. When Mookie met Ty, he looked at me, "He is the one Ms. Lady."

I, in return, rolled my eyes and said, "So you think."

Nitra was a beautiful blushing fifty-something year-old bride who looked and was acting like she was not a day over twenty-five. She danced and had a good time with her guests. Her children were also there and looked close to Mookie's age. They seemed to be one big happy family.

I was most excited to meet Mookie's parents, his brother, and his sister. His mom seemed rather reserved, but his father, sister and brother were outgoing. They told me that they had heard a lot about me and were glad they finally got to meet me. Mookie's sister whispered to me that she thought that Mookie and I were both in denial about our love, and that she thought one day we would realize it and marry. I assured her that we were always the best of friends since "Day One."

She looked at me and said, "I have been married for fifteen years to my best friend and I love him more and more every day. If you don't remember anything else, remember that if you have a great friendship, you will have an even better marriage. Because after the attraction and sex gets old, you will still have your best friend."

Wow, was Mookie's sister really giving me relationship advice. At this point, I am willing to listen to anyone who has been in a longstanding successful relationship. Because up to now, I have had no luck with men.

As I thought about my non-luck with men, I saw Ty getting Mookie's mother up to do the Cupid Shuffle. I watched him work his magic to bring her out of her shell. Once Mookie's mom got on the floor, she stole the show. She was laughing and having a good time with all her children and Ty. I found my camera to videotape the performance. It was the hit of the night.

Ty and I left the wedding reception laughing and talking. He stopped dead in his tracks, and with a serious look on his face said, "I just want to see you happy like this for a lifetime."

"Ty, unfortunately, life is not always going to be a fairy tale. We have to deal with both the ups and downs."

"Yeah, I know, but it just makes me happy to see you happy. I am so sorry I messed us up."

"That was so long ago, Ty. I have forgiven you and moved on."

"Yes, but I would like for us to move on together, not separately."

"I don't know what to say Ty "

"Come here. Don't say anything. Just let me hold you."

I must have been tipsy from the champagne because I complied with his request. I looked up and the sky was full of bright stars.

As I was looking at a falling star, Ty said, "I wish upon a star tonight, that God will bring back together the love that was so right."

He then kissed me and I felt shivers run throughout my body.

I had booked adjoining rooms for Ty and me. When we made it back to the hotel Ty told me he could not stay in an adjoining room, because it would be hard to know that I was just a step away, but he could not hold me throughout the night. He went on to say that he knew that I did not want to sleep with him. I responded by telling him that I was not ready to sleep with anyone.

He looked at me with sad eyes and said, "I understand."

He asked the hotel attendant whether there were any available rooms. The lady found him a room on a different floor. The elevator stopped at Ty's floor first.

He looked at me and said, "Goodnight, Porchia. How I wish you could be in my arms tonight."

I said, "Goodnight, Ty." And in my thoughts, I said, *I would love to be in your arms tonight.* Then the elevator closed.

I knew that this was the last time I would be seeing him on this trip because we were leaving on different flights. Ty had a business trip to Atlanta before returning to Houston to pick up Penny. Oh, how I wished things could be different.

When I woke up the next morning, I was starving. I realized that I had not eaten anything of substance at the reception. I went to breakfast and wished that Ty could have eaten with me. I was in a daze when this tall, dark, handsome bald man, who seemed to be in his forties, walked over to the table and asked if I was alone.

I hesitated before saying, "Yes, I am."

"Well, do you mind if I join you? I am so tired of eating alone."

I did not know what to say so I said, "Sure."

"So, are you on business in Charlotte?" he asked.

"No, I came for a friend's wedding."

"Oh, really. I was here for my ex-wife's wedding."

"Your ex-wife does not happen to be Professor Nitra Thomas?"

He looked at me with a surprised look on his face and said, "No, now she is Professor Nitra Davis."

"Is she changing her name?"

"Yes, she is changing her name. Her new husband thought it was important for her to do so, so she agreed."

"I did not see you at the reception. Just to let you know, I'm here because her new husband is one of my dearest friends."

"You did not see me because I opted not to go, no disrespect to your friend. I think he is a great young man. Yes, with an emphasis on young."

"I guess you don't approve."

"If he makes her happy... Well, you probably know the saying."

"Wow, how did this happen?"

"What happen?" he asked.

"You and I sitting, talking about my best friend and your ex-wife. By the way, you look young also. If you don't mind me asking, how old are you"?"

"I am fifty-nine years old."

"So, you are sitting here with me. Are you interested in me?" I asked.

"No, I am not interested in you, but I do find you attractive. I also know that I could be your father. I would never step over those boundaries."

"So you sat here because you really wanted company?"

"Yes, look around. Is there any other person sitting alone in this restaurant?"

I looked around and he was right. I glanced around at each table and noticed that people were either couples or with a group.

"Well, I am glad you asked. It is no fun eating alone." I said.

"That has been the story of my life, young lady. I just can't seem to find the right lady for me."

"Mr. Thomas, can I ask what you do for a living?"

"Trying to desperately transition into a life of early retirement. However, these days I find myself sitting on various boards for major corporations. But in my real job, I am the owner of Christian Times Inc."

My mouth dropped. Everyone referred to him as Chief, and I did not realize that this was Chief.

"And I am sorry if I have been rude. We just began talking and I did not officially introduce myself officially. I am Christian Thomas. And whose company am I enjoying?"

"It is a pleasure to meet you, Mr. Thomas. I am Porchia Williams DuBois."

"You are shitting me! You are the Porchia Williams DuBois with three best sellers and the host of Straight Talk!"

"That's me, Chief. Why does everyone call you Chief?"

"I was once a Chief Petty Officer in the navy and the name just carried over from those days. It is really an honor to meet you young lady."

"Yeah, I could not have orchestrated this better if I tried," I said laughing.

"So, have you heard that we are working on a deal to air *Straight Talk* in Canada, UK, and Australia?"

"This is the first I have heard of that. I think at this point we need to discuss a salary adjustment," I said laughing.

"Ha! A woman with smarts and a heart. I am sure that is possible, young lady. Approach Larry about that and I will support you."

"That sounds awesome."

"So, when can we expect your fourth book?"

I lied and said, "I am working on it now."

"Great, can't wait to read it."

We talked a little bit more before he said he had to go. He took out his business card and began writing on it. He handed me his card and told me if I ever needed anything, to call him directly on his personal line which he had written on the back of the card.

"Thank you, Mr. Thomas. It was really a pleasure meeting and talking with you."

"Okay, Mr. Thomas was my dad, please call me Chief."

"Will do, Chief. Have a safe journey back home. I believe that is NYC."

"Yes, ma'am, it is. And I believe that you reside in Houston, right?"

"Yes, sir."

"Well, you have a safe trip back to Houston, young lady. And don't hesitate to use that card."

"I won't, sir."

With that, Chief disappeared. I sat thinking about how much of a coincidence could that have really been.

Was God working when I least expected? I then began wondering whether Nitra had anything to do with me getting a job at her husband's company. I took a mental note to ask Mookie whether he knew anything about that.

I left Charlotte in good spirits, realizing that I had just met one of the most powerful black men in media and entertainment. And contrary to how I had pictured him, he was such a down-to-earth brother. I began to wonder what caused him and Nitra to divorce. Obviously, they were still friends since he took time out of his schedule to attend her wedding.

Chapter 20

Ty checked on me to see if I had returned home safely. We had a short conversation because he was in between meetings. He said he would be down in two days to pick up Penny and that Penny requested a date with Sly and me. I started wondering whether Penny was really making these requests. But I thought it would be great to get Sly out of the house.

Recently, Sly had been dreaming and crying out for his mommy in the middle of the night. I told Sweezy we should consider getting him a grief counselor who specialized in counseling children who lost a parent at an early age. To my surprise, Sweezy thought that was a great idea, and contacted some of his associates to find a qualified counselor. I wanted to suggest that he went too, but knew that I should not push him too hard right now. Interestingly enough, the counselor Sweezy chose also required the parent to attend every other session with their child. I smiled when Sweezy told me this. It reminded me of what Aunt Hattie always said, "God is in the prayer-answering business."

****

We arrived at Dave & Buster's before Ty and Penny. Penny and Sly had not seen each other in a while, but Sly immediately recognized her and ran to her saying, "Hi, Penny!" He seemed genuinely excited to see her and she returned the excitement by trying to pick him up and kiss him.

Ty walked over and whispered in my ear, "I wish you would get that excited about seeing me."

I laughed and said, "Do you want me to try to pick you up?"

"Oh, I see you got jokes."

Sly started pulling on my leg saying, "Can we go play?"

Ty handed Penny some money and said, "Watch him closely."

"She does not need to watch me closely, Uncle Ty. I am a big boy," said Sly.

"Yes, you are big guy. But we want to make certain that no one takes you away from us," responded Ty.

"Like God did Mommy?"

Ty looked at me as if to say what should I say, so I chimed in and said, "Yeah, something like that, but Mommy is in a good place. There are some people that would not take you to a good place. So we have to be careful."

"Okay, Teepee. Penny won't let nothing bad happen to me," Sly said with a big smile on his face.

"I will not, but you have to promise to stay close to me at all times," chimed in Penny.

"I will Penny. I promise," responded Sly.

"Princess, you have your phone to call me right?" asked Ty.

"Yes, Brother. I have my phone."

"Is it on?"

Penny sighed, "Yes, it is on Brother."

"Okay, be careful."

I kissed both Sly and Penny then they both took off.

"Now that I have you all to myself. Can I get a kiss?" asked Ty.

I pecked him on his cheek. He looked at me and asked, "Is that all I get?"

"You are such an ingrate!" I pretended to be upset.

He leaned close to my face and said, "I can't wait for you to give me something which I will be forever grateful."

"And what would that be, Mr. Gamble?"

"Your hand in marriage."

"That is a cheap a proposal!"

The hostess walked up to us and said, "Mr. Gamble, your table is ready."

"Oh, you were saved by the bell again," I said.

Ty smiled as he put his hand forward for me to follow the hostess.

Once we were seated, Ty called Penny to tell her where we were sitting so they could join us to order. They showed up within a few minutes. Once they ordered, Sly asked could they go play again until the food came. Ty looked at me and I said, "Sure."

Penny looked at Ty and said, "Brother, I need more money."

"You always need more money Princess. You are going to have to get a job soon." Ty handed Penny forty dollars.

"Anyway I can help out, I will Brother," Penny said with a smile and left with Sly.

I laughed and said, "I see she has you eating out of her hands."

"So do you," Ty said with a boyish grin.

Ty filled me in about some of the things that had been happening with the team and that he was contemplating retirement.

"Are you financially ready to retire?"

"Yes, I am, but I have also been working a deal with a network to broadcast basketball games. I could never see myself not doing anything."

"So why are you contemplating retiring?"

"I am tired of being away from Penny, being on the road, the planes, the hotels, the groupies, the management, the politics, getting banged up, you name it. There are plenty of reasons."

Our food arrived and before Ty could call Penny, she and Sly were walking back to the table.

I looked at Penny and said, "Perfect timing."

"It was actually Sly's idea to come and check to see if the food was here. He said that he was famished," said Penny.

I laughed and said, "Did he say famished?"

"Yes, Teepee. I am famished!" screamed Sly as he sat next to Ty and Penny sat next to me.

Penny said, "Well, shall we say grace?"

"Yes, sweetie, would you like to lead us in grace?" I asked.

Ty shot me a strange look.

She began reciting a grace that made me look up wondering whether she would ever finish. She thanked God for everything, including the sunny, blue sky outside. When she finally finished, I said, "That was a lovely grace Penny."

She smiled and said, "Brother says that my blessings are too long. I don't think there is ever enough time to properly thank God."

"You thank in the manner you think is appropriate," I said.

"She looked at me and said, "Thank you, Pocahontas. You are the best."

I could see Ty rolling his eyes so I said, "Hey, I saw that!"

"Me too," said Penny, while rolling her eyes back at him.

Ty looked at the both of us and said, "I don't think I can stand the eye-rolls from the both of you."

Sly then screamed, "Look, Uncle Ty. I can do it too!" He then attempted to roll his eyes, but instead, stuck them out like Buckwheat.

We all laughed until our food got cold.

I thoroughly enjoyed my meal and the company. Several couples passed by and told Ty that he had a lovely family.

He would smile and say, "Yes, God continues to bless me."

We were there for hours, and Ty was only asked for his autograph three times. Sly looked and said, "Uncle Ty, why do people want you to sign your name?"

"Do you watch sports?"

"Yes, I like football."

"Who is your favorite football player?"

"Uh, me and Daddy like Dez Biant."

"Well, I am a lot of people's favorite player, but I play basketball."

"I have seen basketball," said Sly.

"I play for a team called the Slammers."

"Well, you should play for the Rockets. Me and daddy watch the Rockets."

"Yes, that would be nice. Maybe one day you can come watch me play with my team."

"That would be fun, Uncle Ty. And maybe one day you can watch me play on my team."

"Sounds like a deal li'l man," Ty said while rubbing Sly's head.

Penny looked at me and said, "Sports, sports, sports, all the time. I like music and modern dance. What about you Pocahontas?"

"I like it all. Music, dance, sports," I answered.

"Yes, that is what I love about Pocahontas. She is so well-rounded," Ty said winking at me.

"Are you teasing me because I have gained a couple of pounds Ty?"

"Never that. If you gained fifty pounds, you still would be beautiful in my eyes," responded Ty.

"Flattery will get you nowhere Mister," I said.

Ty and I sat talking and bantering at each other for a while until Penny said, "Oh, boy, there you two go flirting with each other again," said Penny. "Can we go play some more?"

Ty said, "Sure but..."

"Yeah, I know. Make certain I listen for my phone. Thank you," Penny leaned over and kissed me.

Sly said, "I want a kiss too, Teepee."

"Come here Snug Bug."

He came over and I smothered him with kisses and he laughed as usual.

Once they left, Ty looked me directly in my eyes and asked, "What do I have to do to have you be part of our lives forever?"

"Ty, I ain't going nowhere."

"Okay, let me rephrase the question. What do I have to do to get you to marry me?"

"Honestly, I am not sure."

"Do you love me?"

"I don't think I ever stopped loving you."

"So have you forgiven me?" "Yes," I answered.

"Do you trust me?"

"I don't know."

"Okay, I have to earn your trust. At least I know what I should concentrate on."

"It may be easier for us to just concentrate on being good friends."

"I don't want you as my good friend. I want you as my wife."

"Baby steps Ty. Baby steps."

The evening ended with Ty and Penny walking Sly and me to our car. Sly and Penny embraced and said their goodbyes. Ty looked at me and said, "I will earn your trust again, and you will one day be Pocahontas Gamble."

I smiled as he opened my door. I buckled Sly into his car seat and asked, "Did you have fun tonight?"

"Teepee, it was the bestest time. I love Penny and Uncle Ty."

Ty heard him and said, "And I love you and Teepee to the moon and back."

Ty leaned over and kissed me on my forehead. Once I got into my car and Ty closed my door, I said to myself, *and I love you too, Ty.*

Chapter 21

Every week I had a myriad of topics I discussed on Straight Talk, but my all-time favorite discussion was, "How do you trust a person that has previously abused your trust?" It took me a few weeks to convince my broadcasting producer that this subject would interest a lot of callers and my theory proved true.

We received a variety of calls about trust issues that ranged from wives having babies by men that were not their husbands, to a daughter confiding in me that she came to terms with her boyfriend having sex with her father. However, the most compelling story came from an elderly caller. She was a ninety-year-old widow. Initially, I thought I had made a big mistake by taking a call from a ninety-year-old, but she was every bit as lucid as a thirty-year-old.

She told me that she had lost her husband ten years ago, and that when she lost her husband, her eldest son, who loved her dearly, moved in to take care of her. Her son was previously an investment banker, but for some reason he had lost his job. Little did she know, her son was addicted to crack cocaine. She said small things began disappearing from the house. Then she started noticing money and other valuables disappearing. When she approached her son, he told her that she was just a crazy old woman, and that nothing was missing.

She said within weeks of him moving in with her, he would disappear for days at a time. When he returned home, he said that he had been working. One early morning after being gone for two days, he came in telling her that he needed money. She told him that she did not have any money. He told her that he knew that she had money hidden somewhere and she better give it to him, or she would be sorry. The more she told her son that she did not have any money, the angrier he would get, until he finally started slapping and beating her.

According to the ninety-year-old caller, a neighbor found her barely breathing, lying on the floor with the phone next to her. Her son had beat her into unconsciousness. After a few days, the police contacted her to get the story. She told the police what happened, they found her son and arrested him the following day. Her son never went to jail because he took a plea deal where he was given the opportunity to go to a treatment facility instead of jail.

The ninety-year-old woman said, "I wanted that boy to pay for what he did to me. From the time he was born, I gave that boy all of me, anything he wanted was his. I had complete trust in him and loved him dearly. And in return for my love, he almost killed me."

She said God spoke to her and told her to have forgiveness in her heart as He forgives us for all of the sins we commit. The elderly caller said, after about a year, she had forgiven her son, but still did not want to have anything to do with him, because she could never trust him again. The Lord spoke to her again and said, *lean not on you understanding, but trust in Me.* The woman asked the Lord, how could she ever have trust in her son again? The Lord asked in return, did she love her son? She told the Lord, despite what he has done to me, I still love him. The Lord then led her to the verse 1 Corinthians 13:7 that read, *Love bears all things, believes all things, hopes all things, endures all things.*

After the Lord revealed that scripture to her, she prayed that her son would come out a better man, and accept Jesus as his personal Savior. According to the caller, her son was released from his facility two years after going in. She did not hear from the son, but prayed, night after night, that he was living right and doing okay.

She said, the following year she received an anonymous invitation to attend a Christmas celebration at a house on the exquisite side of town. She called and told her daughter she wanted to attend, and would like if she attended with her.

When they arrived at the address, there were luxury cars lined up and down the circular driveway. There was a person waiting to valet park their car. Once they reached the front door, a man dressed in a tuxedo greeted them and took their coats.

As they walked through the door, they saw people dressed in black, serving all of the guests. The guests were all impeccably dressed in formal wear. Her daughter asked, "Mom, who sent you the invite to this bourgeoisie party?"

They were looking around when they heard a voice say, "Mom!" She looked up and her son was standing in a black dress tailcoat tuxedo. He ran over to her and said, "Thank you for coming," and he hugged and kissed her. He also greeted his sister with a kiss.

He told them to stand right there, and he would be right back. He came back with three champagne glasses and a knife. He gave them each a champagne glass, then clicked the knife on his glass and shouted, "Can I have everyone's attention?"

The crowd became quiet. The lady said her son then said, "This party it to honor my mother for the love that she has showered me with over the years. I know that she is a Godly, praying woman, and she is the only reason I am here today. I could never thank her enough for what she has done. In attempt to honor her, I am having this party, and giving her this house, along with a full-time assistant to help clean, cook, and do whatever she needs, as a means of saying thank you Mom. I hope that you know that I would never be able to repay you for the love that you have shown me, this is just a small gesture of the love I have for you. I know as it says in Proverbs, *A wise son makes a glad father, but a foolish son is a sorrow to his mother.* Mom, I am sorry for all of the pain I have caused you, and I hope that one day you will forgive me. Until my dying day, I am going to spend the remainder of my life making you smile."

She said at that time, tears started streaming from her eyes, and the crowd roared with cheers and applause. Never in a million years would she had dreamt about moving into a place like that. Her son had remembered her telling him and his siblings stories when they were little about a beautiful mansion where a princess dwelled. When she looked around the house, she saw that he attempted to recreate the house in her stories.

She said that her son told her that he did not expect her to suddenly believe in him, but he wanted to earn her trust again. 'Til this day, they have the greatest mother-son relationship. He has truly shown that he will be there for her until her dying days. He had established himself once again as one of the top financial investors in the country, and ran a prison ministry group.

She ended our conversation by saying, "My trust did not come from believing in my son, but believing in the promises of God."

After leaving the show an emotional wreck from the woman's story, I went home and prayed for God to lead me in the right direction. I asked God if Ty is the right husband for me, please speak clearly so I will have no doubts.

I told God I would do as the wise elderly lady did, I would no longer lean on my understanding, but on his guidance to answer my prayers. I affirmed my complete faith in Him, and his ability to answer my prayers.

****

Reggie Gobbs, the compensation director with Christian Time Inc., called me to discuss a revision of my current contract. I had not produced my fourth book and thought maybe he wanted to discuss deadlines with me. My lead publisher had not approached me, so I knew it had to be something big if Reggie was contacting me from Corporate.

I flew to NYC the next week to meet with Reggie. To my surprise, it was Reggie, and Larry Mitchell, the President of Broadcasting, in the room. I did not see anyone from the publishing side of the house, so I knew it was unrelated to my book contract.

Reggie thanked me for coming and said that Chief contacted him and Larry to attempt to renegotiate my Straight Talk contract. He went on to say that they wanted to restructure my contract from salaried, to a salary plus a profit sharing compensation package.

I told them this was all foreign to me and I am not certain what they were talking about. Reggie went to the white board and demonstrated what he was talking about. They were primarily offering me twenty percent of the gross made from increasing markets around the world from my show. Reggie showed my total salary package would be well in the seven-digit range.

I asked them what they expected from me. Larry told me that I would have to travel to some of their expanding markets to sell the show and myself. I asked him how much travel would this entail. Larry looked at me with a smirk on his face and said, "The better question is how much time will you be at home?"

I followed up with questions about how soon would I have to travel, and how much time I had to make a decision about whether I was interested in this opportunity. They looked at each other with raised eyebrows, then Larry said to me, "We need for you to start your road trips next month."

Then Reggie chimed in and said, "You have until next week to give us your decision."

"And if I want to keep my same contract, what happens?" I asked.

They looked at each other with a puzzled looked on their faces, then both stared at me for what seemed like forever. Then Larry finally said, "Well, since Chief insisted that we approach you with this, you probably need to talk with him if you decide not to take it."

I left NYC not certain how I felt. I was happy about the chance of making millions in salary, but it seemed like they were asking a lot from me. Additionally, how could I leave Sly and Sweezy? Was this God's way of letting me know that Ty was not the one for me?

The entire plane ride my head was spinning with all sort of thoughts. I kept hearing Aunt Hattie's voice saying, "Baby Girl, God comes first, with family not far behind." By the time I landed, I decided to call Chief and have a discussion with him to feel him out.

Chapter 22

My first priority was checking on Sweezy and Sly. Sweezy seemed to take his primary role as a caretaker very seriously. Their counseling sessions seemed to be helping both of them deal with Mystery's death. Sly stopped having nightmares, and Sweezy kept busy working on Mommy's Haven. I don't think he had time to think about his loss.

Sly asked me to put him to bed and read a Bible story. After reading him a couple of chapters, he fell fast asleep. I went to look for Sweezy to discuss the business proposal I was offered. I found Sweezy in the office working on paperwork for Mommy's Haven. I had not been as involved lately as I would have liked to have been, but Sweezy was expertly handling the non-profit, as he had with his other business ventures.

After we discussed the progress that they were making on opening three homes, I told him about my job offer. Sweezy told me that he would be upset if I even thought about turning down the job offer because of him and Sly. I told him that the job would require me to do a lot of traveling, including a lot of overseas travel, and I did not want to be away from home that long.

Sweezy looked at me and asked, "Why Swoosh? You have no responsibilities here that would prevent you from being mobile and pursuing an offer of a lifetime."

"Yes, I do. I have you, Sly, Mommy's Haven, Chardonnay, and..."

"Stop! You are making excuses. I have all of that under control. We are a family, and we pitch in to help each other in times of need. I promise, I will take care of everything while you're gone, including Chardonnay."

"By the way, why didn't you tell me that Chardonnay had a girlfriend?"

"Oh, so she finally told you?"

"No, I walked in on them."

Sweezy laughed and said, "Ah, you walked in on them bumper-to-bumper."

"That is not funny, Sweezy, I was caught totally off guard."

"I did not tell you because it is none of my business who Chardonnay sleeps with."

"Well, anyway, Roni seems like she is a nice person. I just hope that she does not hurt her."

"Chardonnay can definitely take care of herself when it comes to the romances and the finances. Swoosh, you need to just concentrate on what you'd like to do. You're always worried about others."

"Family comes first with me, Sweezy."

"But if you can't take care of yourself, you can't take care of family."

"Taking care of myself does not mean I need a seven-digit income."

"Well, what would you like?"

"For everyone around me to be happy."

"And what about your happiness?"

"That's it, when I see that you all are doing well, I'm happy."

"Swoosh, you need to be honest about what you want. Your life should not be dependent on the happiness of others. It's okay for it to be about you sometimes. Why don't you try this exercise that I did as part of my counseling. Write down five things you want to achieve in the next five years. This will help you focus on what is most important to you."

"Oh, now you're giving me homework."

"No, I am asking you to think about what you want. Humor me."

"Okay, Pappa Sweezy, I will do that. Hey, I think I am going to crash over here. Is that okay?"

"You know this house is your house too."

"I have not paid any mortgage."

"Me neither." Sweezy said smiling.

"Oh, sorry. I forgot Pappa Money Bag paid for his house in cash."

"Ah Swoosh, don't hate da player."

"Oh, now you a player, huh? A'ight, player, I am going to make my way to my room," I said punching him lightly on his arm.

"Cool, and don't forget your homework."

"Okay, Professor."

I went to my room and seriously began thinking about what I wanted. I took out my tablet and wrote, Five Year Goals. That is as far as I got before I drifted off to sleep.

****

I woke up to the phone ringing. Ty called asking me if I was ready for the trip next month. I had completely forgotten that I was supposed to go with him and Penny to Paradise Island. He told me Penny's entire conversation was about her birthday trip, once he accidentally slipped and told her that I was joining them.

I told Ty that I may have a conflict, but I would know within the next few days whether I would be able to make the trip. Ty's conversation started upbeat, but when I shared the news that I may not be able to make it, the flow of the conversation changed. Ty finally came out and asked what type of conflict I had that would prevent me from attending Penny's birthday celebration. I shared with Ty the conversation that I had with the management team from Christian Times Inc.

Ty became excited again and thought that it would be an opportunity of a lifetime. He informed me that his contract ended, and that he decided not to renew; so he possibly could travel with me if I would like. He also informed me that he had planned on moving to Houston after Penny finished the school year.

He downloaded so much information on me in such a short time frame that my head was spinning. He also threw in the fact that it would be great for Penny and Sly to be able to spend more time together. Since Penny had also lost both of her parents at a young age, she could assist Sly through his loss.

I told Ty that I still had to think about whether I wanted to take the job, and frankly, just think about life in general. I needed to decide what was best for me, and that I would be listening to God for guidance.

After I finished my speech, geared toward letting Ty know that he needed to slow down, he said, "I am not going to give up hope on us ever again, Pocahontas. God has revealed to me that you are the one for me."

I could not resist bringing up the elephant in the room so I asked, "Have you stopped sleeping with men?"

"I have not been involved sexually with anyone in a long time."

"Well, have you had the urge to sleep with men?"

"I don't have the urge to sleep with anyone but you, Pocahontas. I want to be honest with you, when I married Jill, I had sex with a man after making love to Jill. I am ashamed of that, but she was not the one for me. Every other woman that I am with I compare them to you. Porchia, when I say that I want you and no other man or woman, I mean it. If it is not you, it will not be anyone."

"I just don't understand how you can be so certain?"

"Well, let me ask you this. Have there been others in your life that you wanted to call your husband?"

"No, I have not."

"Why is that, Pocahontas? Before you answer, please be honest with me, but more importantly, be honest with yourself."

There was a long pause before I responded, "Because, I have not met anyone that makes me feel, the way that you make me feel."

Chapter 23

I called Chief to have a heart-to-heart conversation with him. I told him everything that was going on in my life, and he said, "Porchia, I think you need time to just chill. Don't worry about the deadline that we put on you. How about you take until the first of the year to decide what is best for you. I can't have you out there if your head is not into what you are doing. One of the keys to success is loving what you do, and right now, I can tell that you're conflicted."

I thanked Chief for believing in me and giving me the opportunity to lead his endeavor. I also let him know that I appreciated the additional time to figure out my direction in life.

I was so happy after my conversation with Chief, I immediately called Ty to let him know that I would be able to make Penny's birthday trip. He informed me that Penny's best friend would also be coming, and she asked whether Sly could join in as well. I told him that I would run it by Sweezy to see if he would be willing to let Sly go.

When I asked Sweezy, he thought it was a great idea, and he wanted to join in on the celebration as well. The birthday trip for three, turned into a long weekend birthday celebration of seven. I was excited because this would have been the first time that we had taken Sly on a vacation, and the first time that Sweezy would get away from Houston since Mystery's death.

****

I was buried with work for the entire month. Although I was given until January to decide on whether I would take on the additional responsibilities, I researched different areas that may be open to talk radio.

I found out that in addition to Europe, particularly Israel was a hot spot for expansion. I signed up to take several language courses that I thought would help me if I decided to branch out into other countries. I would have a translator for the countries where I did not understand the language, but I thought it would be prudent for me to understand the conversational basics.

I was already fluent in Spanish and French, so I decided to add Arabic, Hebrew, Italian, and Portuguese to my repertoire of foreign languages spoken. I signed up for Italian and Portuguese simultaneously; and took Arabic and Hebrew separately, since I figured they would be the most difficult for me to master. I also signed up for a cultural etiquette course to assist me in understanding what is and is not acceptable in various countries, especially in the Middle East and Asia, where I was most interested in expanding my broadcast, because of the historical unfair and unequal distinctions made between men and women.

160

Once I started my research and saw some of the gender issues, I was ready to go to the Middle East and Asia to start the discussion on various inequalities. Inequalities such as women not having the right to drive in Saudi Arabia; women not having the right to divorce in Lebanon without an eyewitness to an injustice; women not having the right to education in Afghanistan; and women in Pakistan not having the right to choose whom they will marry.

I approached Larry Mitchell to tell him about my ideas, and he told me that I would be entering into some topics that were taboo in the Middle East and Asia and based on religious practices. Additionally, he informed me that it would be illegal to even broadcast such topics in certain countries.

I asked him whether he would support me if I could find an area where it is not taboo to discuss, and there was a possibility of increased listenership in areas that were not currently exposed to such topics for public discussion. He said he would wait for my proposal before saying "yay or nay".

I was looking forward to making an impact on some of the mistreatment of people across the world. I knew that I could positively contribute to a conversation about human rights. I poured a lot of time and research and decided that United Arab Emirates and Qatar would be great spots to start discussions around these issues. Both countries, although heavily populated with Muslims, were not as conservative as their surrounding countries. In addition, I could reach other countries that were in close proximity to UAE and Qatar that had serious issues as it relates to women's rights. I knew that I would also have to hit some of the European nations, so I decided that UK, Italy and France were also ripe for various dialogue at a later date. I poured hours into my presentation and perfected both my visual and oral presentation skills.

I ran my ideas by Sweezy and Auntie Char, and neither one of them seemed to be receptive to me going to the Middle East. I also spoke to Ty about it, and he was supportive of anything that I wanted to do, but he did not necessarily feel that the Middle East was the safest place for me to be alone. I tried to convince them that I would not be traveling to Syria, Afghanistan, Pakistan, Iran or Iraq, but would stay in the safer zones. According to Sweezy, there was all sort of dangers within the Middle East and parts of Asia, that as Americans, we were not exposed.

I asked Larry to explore options, specifically for Dubai and Doha, to see if there were restrictions that would prevent us from broadcasting within those two cities. In addition, after establishing our audience, would it be possible to stream from America to those countries.

Larry told me that I did not have to worry about if it could be done, that he would work on how it will be done. He had connections in Dubai that could easily assist him in getting whatever was necessary for Dubai. According to Larry, once we set up in Dubai, Qatar would be a "cake walk." He only needed to be convinced that the effort would be worth it.

Sweezy, after finding out that I was interested in going to the Middle East, asked me whether I had completed my list of what I wanted to accomplish in the next five years. I decided that before making a final decision on whether I would take on my new venture, I owed it to myself to make the list. After three days of asking myself some tough questions and doing a critical self analysis, I wrote the following:

Follow God's mission

Be an important part of Sly's life

Get married

Make a significant contribution to the world

Expand Mommy's Haven

I had to laugh when I reviewed my list. The list seemed a little aggressive for a five-year plan. But I knew whatever I set my mind to do, I could achieve. The one thing that seemed the most unattainable is getting married, because I did not even have a suitor besides Ty.

When I really examined what I was saying, I realized that my goal was to either be with Ty, or let him go forever, so that we could both find someone to spend the rest of our lives with. After years of trying, I knew it was impossible for us to be *just* friends.

After spending weeks of planning the rest of my life, I was looking forward to the little break to Paradise Island. I was going to take the opportunity to just rest and relax, because I realized once I made it back to Houston, I would be on the run making my five year plan a reality.

Chapter 24

On the day I was departing for Paradise Island, Auntie Char let me know that she was a little sour that we did not include her in on our family vacation. I explained to her that it was Penny's birthday, and Ty invited Sly and me; however, Sweezy would not allow Sly to travel without him by his side.

I told her it would be great if we all, including Roni, planned something for Thanksgiving away from Houston. Auntie Char thought it would be a great idea, and she would check in with Roni to see if she was down.

The day that we were leaving, Sly came down with a fever, so Sweezy decided that it was best if they did not go. Sly cried for hours, until I told him about the family trip that we would all take when I got back.

Before I left out the door, Sly looked at me with a sad look and tears rolling down his face and said, "Teepee, I already miss you sooo much." I told him that I would miss him and would bring him something special back. He came and hugged my leg and I bent down and gave him sloppy kisses, which made him laugh.

I met Ty and his crew in Miami. When Penny saw me, her eyes lit up and she said, "Thank you so much for coming Pocahontas. Brother said he was not sure you would make it, but I told him that I knew that you would make it."

"There is no other place I would rather be than celebrating your first teenage birthday with you."

She grabbed my hand and said, "Come on, you have to meet my bestie, Kel."

Kel seemed to be very opposite of Penny. Penny was very outgoing and extroverted; whereas, Kel seemed to be more reserved and quiet. I made a note to keep an eye on her, because my experience taught me that the quiet ones are usually the wild ones.

Ty just stood back and observed the whole interaction. When I looked up, he smiled and reached out his hand to me and said, "You look lovely, Pocahontas."

I grabbed his hand, gave him a smile, and said, "You don't look bad yourself, Mr. Gamble."

"I will feel so much better when I am able to call you Mrs. Gamble."

"Ty, can we make this vacation stressless?"

"Oh, do I stress you?"

"Yes, when you make remarks such as that."

"Okay, I will try to make it as stressless on you as I can," he said, blushing and exposing his white teeth and dimples against his creamy chocolate skin.

I started wondering why after all of these years, I still get a physical reaction when he smiles, touches me, flirts, and whatever else he does. I thought to myself, *This will be a long weekend.* Ty and I sat next to each other, and the girls sat across the aisle from us. The flight attendant recognized Ty and said, "Oh, it's great that you are taking a vacation with your family."

Both Ty and I just smiled and told her what we wanted to drink. The girls ordered soda, and Ty looked at Penny and told her that she needed something without caffeine and little sugar. She changed her drink to cranberry juice, while Kelly ordered a Diet Coke.

I whispered to Ty that I thought he was being a little tough on her, and he informed me that she breaks out when she has too much caffeine or sugar. He swore that she would have a mental crash if her face broke out during vacation. He went on to tell me how vain she was about her appearance, but still wanted to indulge in things that were not good for her.

I looked at him and told him that some things she would have to learn on her own, and that he could not be around to direct all of her moves. He convinced me that he was just trying to remain sane, because her breakdowns could sometimes be extreme, and he did not have the energy to deal with one of her meltdowns while on vacation. He said he was very much looking forward to downloading during this time. I told him that I felt the same way, and was glad that I had agreed to join them.

Before I realized it, we hand landed in the Bahamas and were on our way to Paradise Island. When we arrived at the villa, I was totally taken aback at the six bedroom, six-bath mini-mansion that Ty rented. The humongous, fully staffed villa included a butler, chef, housekeeper, and driver, and was situated right on the beach with an oversized infinity pool.

Since Sweezy and Sly did not join us, we had three unused bedrooms because the girls opted to stay in a room together that had two beds. We were minutes away from the Atlantis Resort, so Ty purchased a package where we also had full use of the resort.

The girls requested that we do a spa day at Atlantis, so I made plans for a day of pampering. We had mud baths, body scrubs, massages, and facials, accompanied by a full, four course lunch. There were chocolate strawberries, champagne, and sparkling cider that was free flowing throughout the experience.

I came out of the spa feeling like a new woman. The girls were turnt up after their spa treatments, and wanted to partake in the water activities offered at Atlantis. I opted to do some reading and sunbathing. I was relaxing when I heard a voice from behind me say, "Hey, beautiful, can I join you?"

I looked back, and it was Ty, wearing a white linen short set. He looked like a tall chocolate M&M dressed in white. I had to give him a second look, because he seemed to have more muscles than I remembered. I also noticed several women, and some men, were also checking him out. I knew that he noticed people staring, so I said, "Of course you can handsome. But I might be blocking some of your action."

"Pocahontas, the only action I want is from you."

"There you go, getting fresh with me again."

"I apologize, that's just what you do to me."

"Do you have trunks under those shorts?"

"Yeah, my birthday suit contains a big trunk."

"Don't flatter yourself."

"If I don't, I know you won't," Ty said flashing his pearly whites.

"So you come to the pool with no intent to swim?"

"I came looking for you."

The server came by and asked Ty if he would like a drink. He looked at me and said, "What are you drinking?"

"A Pina Colada."

"Let me have what the lady is drinking."

The waiter wrote it down and said, 'I will be back with your drink, sir."

We sat around drinking and talking for several hours until I told Ty that I was a little worried about the girls. They had been gone for a while. He asked where they were and I told them at the waterpark. He said, "Stay here, I will go find them."

"No, I will go with you, or I will be looking for you next."

We searched for the girls for a while. I noticed that Ty became nervous. He went over to one of the lifeguards and gave a description of the girls. The lifeguard said that he had not seen them.

Just as we were going to go into the hotel, we saw Kelly twerking in the middle of two older white guys, who looked like they were about our age, and Penny standing back clapping and laughing. Before I could do or say anything, Ty ran up to one of the guys and grabbed him by his collar and said, "What the fuck are you doing?"

The guy reacted by saying, "Man, what the fuck is wrong with you?"

"Why are you with these thirteen-year-olds?"

His friend chimed in and said, "They said they were eighteen. Lighten up dude, we did not know."

I ran to Ty and said, "Baby, calm down."

"No, these muthafuckas could tell that these girls were young. If you all did anything with them, I will kill you!"

"Ty! Calm down!" I screamed.

Then Penny began crying, "I am sorry, Brother."

"Penny, I am not talking to you right now. I will deal with you later!" yelled Ty.

The guy that Ty had in a chokehold started gasping for air.

I frantically pleaded, "Ty, please let him go!"

"Brother, please! Please stop!"

Ty finally released his grip and the guy said while coughing, "I swear, we did not do anything with them. We were just having some fun, drinking, talking and dancing."

I interjected and said, "Drinking?"

Kelly said, "No, it was soda."

"Ty, I think we need to handle this back at the villa," I said.

Ty pointed at both of the young men and said, 'If I find out that you all did anything harmful to them, I will find you, and you all will be dealt with!"

The man that Ty choked said, "We did not do anything. But you almost killed me!"

Ty got in the man's face and said, "That was nothing compared to what will happen if I find out you did anything to hurt my sister or her friend."

I walked up to Ty and said, "Come on, Ty, let's get the girls back to the villa."

Penny was holding her head down, while Kelly looked like the cat that swallowed the canary. Something told me that this whole ordeal was Kelly's idea. We caught her performing for the guys and I think she also lied about not having anything but soda to drink. I decided I would speak to Penny later without Kelly being around. We all rode back to the villa without anyone uttering a word.

When we arrived, Ty said, "I want you to each have your own room. I will deal with each of you separately. Penny, you will take the room next to me, and Kelly, you will stay in the room that you slept in last night. Please go to your respective rooms until I get you."

Kelly got out of the car upset and stomped into the house. Penny looked at Ty, then me, and said, "I am so sorry for causing you to worry. Nothing like this will ever happen again."

Ty said, "You dayum right it won't. Go to your room until I am ready to discuss this with you."

Chapter 25

Ty was very upset. He confided in me that he was not really certain how to deal with the issue. He also said he knew that he could not pick out Penny's friends, but even before this happened, he felt that Kelly was probably a bad influence on her. He went on to say that Kelly's parents did not discipline her the way that he disciplined Penny. He said, "You know, white folks just don't do like we do."

"Ty, I am not certain it is a black or white thing."

"Yeah, well, I know where I am from. Penny would have gotten her ass beat for pulling a stunt like that."

Marlena, the housekeeper, interrupted us and asked if we needed anything before she returned to her quarters for the night. Ty quickly dismissed her and looked at me as if he forgot what he was going to say.

I picked up where he left off by saying, "Well, I don't necessarily think that beating your child is the best form of discipline."

Ty quickly responded, "Yeah, but Kelly's parents don't parent at all. She has the freedom to do what she wants, when she wants. That is why I don't allow Penny to go and spend the night over there. They don't even check on Kelly when she spends the weekend with us. I am a single man and could be doing anything and everything. And there is no way in hell I would ever let her go on vacation with them. They allow her too much liberty and who knows what the hell she is accustomed to doing. Did you see her twerking better than a stripper? And no, I will not beat Penny, but she would be punished in some form or fashion. She will not be another black statistic."

"I understand your concern, but there is a way that you can do that without being so punitive. She needs to understand what she did, understand that it is unacceptable, and that there are repercussions for unacceptable behavior. Have you spoken with her about sex?"

"Uh, no, I would not even know how to approach that discussion."

"Ty, she is thirteen. Has she started her menstrual cycle yet?"

"I don't know. If she has, her nanny deals with all of that."

"Well, if you like, I can have a talk with her."

"I know that you were hoping this would be a stressless vacation. I am sorry that it has not been so far, but I definitely need your help."

"No problem, Ty, it would be my pleasure to help. I never thought about it, but as a male, it must be difficult raising a girl alone."

"I love her. I want the best for her, but I'm not certain that I am properly equipped to raise her right."

"Ty, you have a lot of love, and I am confident in your abilities. You will always seek to do the right thing."

"I hope so, Pocahontas."

We were interrupted by my phone. I answered and heard, "Hi, Teepee. Are you having fun?

"Hi, Snug Bug, I am. How are you feeling?"

"I feel better now. I wanted to sing Happy Birthday to Penny."

I looked at Ty and said, "Sure, I will let you speak to her now."

I left Ty and went to Penny's room and handed her the phone. I told her to bring it back to me when she was done.

I went back to join Ty and said, "Would you like to have a joint conversation with her when she brings back my phone?"

"I'm not certain I'm ready."

"Well, I know that you probably should not let too much time lapse before you have a discussion with her about what happened."

"Let's go for it."

Within about ten minutes, Penny walked into the room with a sad look on her face. She looked at me and said, "Thank you so much for letting me speak with Sly."

"No problem, sweetie," I said.

She began to walk away and Ty said, "Wait a minute Princess. We would like to speak with you."

She hesitated before turning around. Ty and I were sitting on the sofa and he moved over and pointed to the middle of the sofa and said, "Sit here. First, I want to let you know that I love you and only want the best for you."

Penny said, "I know, Brother. I owe you both an apology. I know what I did today was wrong."

"Why did you do it then?" asked Ty.

"Just thought it would be fun to do something different on my birthday."

"Did you realize those guys are adults and you are still a child?"

"Yes Brother, I did."

"And do you know that they could go to jail for hanging out with you."

"No."

"So what happened? How did you end up with them?" asked Ty.

"Well, Kel and I were just sitting and talking. They came over and asked us how we were doing. Kel told them that we were just celebrating my eighteenth birthday. They then asked why are we celebrating without any drinks and offered to buy us some drinks. So we went to the hotel bar with them and we drank a Bama Mama."

I laughed and said, "You mean, a Bahama Mama?"

"Yeah, something like that. It tasted like punch. So I drank it fast and they offered me another one."

"Had you drank alcohol before?" asked Ty.

"No, Brother. But after the second drink, I started to feel a little dizzy. I told Kel that we needed to find Pocahontas so we can make it back to the villa because I was not feeling well. Kel said that we would leave in a little while and the guys said it was too early to leave the party. That is when Kel started dancing, and that is when you found us."

"Okay, first, drinking alcohol as a minor is not acceptable under any circumstance. Second, being with older guys is not acceptable either. They could have taken advantage of you, especially since you had been drinking. And the way Kelly was dancing is never acceptable!" shouted Ty.

I interjected, "Penny, has anyone spoken with you about sex?"

"Patrice talked about it with me when I was like eight years old. I remember her sharing a book about sex. We also spoke about abuse and how to protect myself against child predators."

"So, I don't know if you know it or not, but there is no way those guys thought you were eighteen. So they are considered child predators. And even though they did not have any type of sexual contact with you, they are guilty of aiding and abetting a minor in alcohol consumption. And those guys know that alcohol limits one's ability to think coherently," I said.

Penny looked shocked and said, "But they seemed very nice. They both were pre-med students."

"Penny, looks can be deceiving, and they could have been lying. You should never put yourself in danger like that," I said.

Ty said, "You know what happens when you have sex, right?"

"Yes, Brother. Unprotected sex can lead to diseases and pregnancy."

"And you don't want to get pregnant or a disease. disease. Cuz if the disease don't kill you, I will," said Ty.

Penny looked distraught, so I interjected and said, "Your brother would never kill you, but you would be ruining your life. You have a whole life ahead of you. You have plenty of time for boys, sex, and whatever else comes with that," I said.

Ty said, "Yes, and you should not even think about sex until you are about thirty-five years old."

I laughed and said, "Yeah, like you did?"

Penny looked at Ty and said, "You are not even thirty-five. So, does that mean you have not had sex?"

"It is not about me young lady, we are talking about you!" Ty shouted.

I attempted to diffuse the situation by saying, "What your brother is attempting to say is that when you enter that period of your life, which should be a long time from now, you need to be sure about the person you have sex with. You should love him enough to want to share your body with him. And even then, you should make certain you are protected against any diseases, and definitely pregnancy. Ideally, you want to choose the right man to love, marry, then have sex, and eventually children. Of course, before all that, we would hope that you have attended college, traveled, enjoyed life, and have a career where you are able to take care of yourself."

Penny paused and said, "Well, by the looks of it, you and Ty should be at that point by now. Why have you not married and had children?"

I looked at Ty and for the first time he was smiling. I quickly responded before Ty broke out with any type of smart comment and said, "Penny, this conversation is about you, not me or your brother. Do you have any questions related to what we have discussed and our concerns for you?"

"No, I understand. I understand that it was wrong lying about our age, drinking, and just going along with the crowd," Penny said.

Ty said, "Okay, based on what you have done. What do you think should be the repercussion?

"I am not certain what are repercussions," said Penny.

"Penny, you know exactly what I am talking about. But if you want me to break it down, how should you be punished?" said Ty.

"Well, since we are here for my birthday, I think my punishment should be deferred until we return home. Once home, I think that I should not be allowed to communicate on any electronic device for a week, and that includes my phone."

Ty looked at Penny and said, "I tell you what, take this as a lesson learned. And if you ever do anything like this again, including lying and drinking, you will not be allowed to do anything but go to school and come back home for a month."

"A month?" screamed Penny

"Keep talking, and the time may go up to the entire school year. And I will be talking with Kelly's parents."

"Okay, can I move back in with Kel?"

"No, I think it is best for you two to keep your separate rooms."

"Brother!"

"Look Penny, don't push me or I will put Kelly in another house!"

"Okay. Will we be able to go to the teen dance at the hotel tonight?"

"Hell no, you can't go!"

I looked at Ty with a look of disapproval on my face.

He then responded, "Okay, you can but Pocahontas and I will keep close dibs on you two. And I expect you to dance like ladies. No twerking or whatever other inappropriate dances you kids do these days! I will also trust you to be responsible from here on out."

"Yes Brother, I will. And I appreciate you both loving me enough to have this discussion. I know this must not be easy for you."

"You are welcome Princess. Just don't let me down," Ty said.

"I won't," she said as she reached over to hug him, and then hugged me and said, "I love both of you."

In unison, Ty and I said, "We love you too!"

Chapter 26

After returning from Penny's birthday trip, Tracy begged me to come and visit her in Vegas. I had promised a family trip to Sly, so I asked Sweezy and Chardonnay if they minded taking a trip to Vegas. Sweezy told me that he was hoping that we would take a trip to the beach house in Puerto Vallarta.

We came up with a compromise. We decided that we would take a two-week vacation, spend one week in Vegas, and one week in Puerto Vallarta. I wanted to make reservations at Mandalay Bay because I knew Sly would enjoy the aquarium they had there. But Tracy talked us into staying with them. She said they had a five-bedroom house that could accommodate everyone.

When we arrived, I was unprepared for what I saw. Tracy's description of a five-bedroom house was inadequate. We drove up to a spectacular gated community that consisted of mansions. Javier's house was probably the most modest on the block, but it was an extremely large home with an Italian-tiled driveway. As we pulled into the circular driveway Sweezy asked, "Are you sure we have the right address?"

Once inside the home, I found it absolutely gorgeous. It had custom features, elaborate art, and unique furnishings in every room. Every bedroom had a different theme. I was a little uncomfortable because I knew that Sly could be a little active, and did not want him to break anything; even though his father probably could pay for it.

Tracy's boyfriend, Javier, was very welcoming and charming. He made everyone feel at home, but paid special attention to Sly. Sly could not say Javier, so he told him to call him Uncle J. This was the first time I witnessed Sweezy having a Mystery moment. I noticed that Sweezy seemed a little envious that Sly was so comfortable around another man.

Sweezy was accustomed to being the only man that Sly looked up to. He found different reasons to take Sly away when he was having too much fun with Uncle J; similar to the way that Mystery acted toward me when she thought I was spending too much time with Auntie Char.

I noticed a dynamic change in Tracy. She seemed to be more confident about herself, than I had witnessed in a long time. Previously, she seemed to have a lot of pretentiousness about her; which I felt was a cover-up for how she really felt about herself.

I observed the way that Javier treated her. He provided her with the love that she had missed from a man her entire life. He was very caring and attentive to her needs, and in return, she was very loving and attentive toward him. However, I was somewhat worried because Tracy had no skills to take care of herself if something happened between her and Javier.

I had the opportunity to speak with her about her goals and objectives in life. She told me that she was happy for the very first time in her life. If it did not work out, that would be fine with her because she had the opportunity to truly understand love and to experience happiness.

"Sister, I did a lot of smiling on the outside, while I was crying on the inside. Now I am smiling from the inside, out. And whatever happens, I will always remember what I experienced during this time. I have learned that I am worthy of being loved the right way."

I told her that I was proud of her, and that she was able to accept love because she was able to love herself. I said, "It is good to embrace Mookie's concept of love."

"What's that?" Tracy asked.

"Girl, Mookie always said, "If loving me is wrong, I don't want to be right."

We both laughed, and then hugged, until we were interrupted by Sly telling us it was time to play a family game of Monopoly.

We had fun as a family. I just wished that Auntie Char and Roni would have stayed with us, but they opted to stay at a hotel on the strip. This would have been my first opportunity to really get to know Roni. However, Auntie Char told me that she did not want to confuse Sly about their relationship. I thought that this was odd because Sweezy only had four bedrooms in Puerto Vallarta, and

Sweezy always insisted that Sly had his own room; so they would end up sleeping together anyway.

The real reason came to light the night before leaving Vegas. On the last night, we had a family dinner. Auntie Char and Roni agreed to join us. They announced that they had gotten married. I was happy for them, but disappointed that I was not included in the nuptials.

I spoke privately with Auntie Char about my disappointment, but she said, they wanted a private ceremony with just the two of them. I had to accept what they desired. After their announcement, Javier arranged for a celebration by providing a cake that said "Congratulation to the Newlyweds" and he purchased two bottles of Dom Perignon for a toast.

Remembering the moment, and thinking about the entire group, it seemed that Sly was the most excited about their marriage. He said, "Tee Char, I am so glad that you are now married. Now we just need to get Teepee to marry Uncle Ty."

I found it amazing how kids are so accepting. He made no distinction between Chardonnay marrying a woman, instead of a man. But as smart as he was, I thought he may need some help in understanding that Uncle Ty and I were not ever going to get married.

When we arrived in Mexico, I noticed a change in Sweezy's attitude. Overall, he was light-hearted when we were in Vegas. However, on the first night at the beach house, I found him sitting outside alone with a Negra Modelo in his hand. I walked up to him and said,

"What's up Pops? You have been quiet since we arrived in Puerto Vallarta."

"Just thinking."

"Yes, I could tell that. But what's up?"

"I have not been here without Queen. The first time we came here, I had just bought the house and I brought her here. We were not even dating then."

"Oh, I did not know that."

"Yeah, and I am just thinking about all of the times we snuck here to get away from Houston without anyone really knowing where we were going. We called it, "The Nookie Spot.""

"The Nookie Spot?"

"Yeah, we snuck here to get our freak on. As a matter of fact, this is where li'l man was conceived."

"Okay, spare me the details!"

"I miss her so much Swoosh."

"Yeah, I miss her too."

"The only thing that is keeping me strong is li'l man."

"Sweezy, I don't have to go to Dubai. I can stay here for you and Sly."

"No, I don't want you to do that. You have to live your life."

"I can live my life right here in Houston."

"Yeah, but there is a reason you chose to go to Dubai."

"I just want women's voices to be heard in that part of the world."

"Then, you gotta do that."

"But, family is first."

"Swoosh, I got this. Everything will be fine. I know the journey won't be easy. But we will get through. As Big John use to say, this too shall pass."

"Well, I could be around to make it easier."

"Actually, you make it more difficult."

"What?"

"Yeah, every time I look at your big head, I think of your mom's big head."

I laughed, popped him on the back on his head and said, "Forget you, Pappa Sylvester!"

Chapter 27

I was busily preparing for my departure to Dubai, I did not have the opportunity to return the many messages that Ty had left for me. Although I had spoken to Penny, I realized that Ty and I had not spoken since we returned from Penny's birthday party.

When I finally called him, he seemed excited to hear from me. He told me that the guy in the Bahamas had filed an assault charge against him; but the case was summarily dismissed by a judge when the judge found out that they were hanging with thirteen-year-old girls. We went on talking about what was going on in his life. However, when I told Ty that I was moving to Dubai, the conversation went silent.

"Ty, are you still there?"

"Why?"

"Why, what?"

"Why did you not talk to me about it before making a decision to move to Dubai?"

"Everything happened so fast. I am starting a talk show there that will be primarily dedicated to the discriminatory treatment of women in Arabic and Islamic countries."

"I guess there really is no chance for us."

I went silent this time. Not certain how to answer. I finally said, "I am doing something that I feel passionate about."

"I am passionate about us being together. Does that matter?"

"Ty, I feel like we have been here before."

"Yes, many times. Are you telling me to give up?"

"I am telling you that this is something I have to do."

"Well, Porchia, I wish you much success in your endeavors."

"Thanks Ty, hopefully we will stay in contact."

"I'm not certain why we would remain in contact."

"I thought we were friends. And I would never turn my back on Penny."

"I am not asking you to turn your back on Penny. But I'm through chasing a pipe dream."

"I am sorry that you feel that way."

"No, I am sorry that you don't feel the same way about me that I feel about you. Bye, Porchia." And with that, our conversation ended.

I was disappointed in Ty's reaction. Even though I doubted that we could carry on a meaningful relationship as friends, I never really imagined him gone from my life forever. But I was committed to doing what I needed to do. I knew that women's voices needed to be heard in that part of the world, and I could be the one to make it happen.

I left Houston a little disheartened. I had to deal with a lot of crying from Sly, sadness from Chardonnay, distance from Sweezy, and a total disconnect from Ty. Two days before my departure, I almost decided to stay, until Sweezy and I had a heart-to-heart conversation. He admitted that he would miss me, but he knew that I would not forgive myself if I did not follow what I felt was my destiny. I assured him that this assignment would only last for about a year, and that I would be back before he had the opportunity to miss me.

I left on a red-eye out of Houston because I knew that I had a sixteen-hour flight ahead of me. If I could get at least six hours sleep during the night that meant that I would only have ten hours remaining.

When we landed in Dubai, I was just amazed at this oasis in the dessert. The city reminded me of an ol' skool cartoon that I once saw called the Jetsons. It was like NYC on steroids, but even more futuristic looking. The thing that most stood out to me was the friendliness of all the people I ran across.

The company arranged for me to stay in corporate housing, which I expected to be an apartment; but I was placed in a four bedroom, five bath home in a gated community with a housekeeper, chef, and driver. I immediately thought I had made a great decision.

I met the station staff, which was comprised of about forty people, and was surprised to find out the only woman at the station was the receptionist, and the only other black person, was an African man from London, who served as a recording engineer. However, everyone

189

treated me as if I were royalty. The producer of my show, Abbas, was a Muslim with very liberal views. He was excited about the topics that we were going to discuss, and said it was time to shake up the Arabic and Islamic communities.

Our first show was about a woman's inability to drive in Saudi Arabia. We had some very vocal views on both sides of the table. The number of men callers that also objected to the treatment that women received in Saudi Arabia pleasantly surprised me.

However, when we discussed the division of women and men in the Islamic community, it caused a lot of controversy. Upon leaving the show that evening, there were demonstrators surrounding the station with signs reading, "In the Name of Allah. Go Away Western Devils." Habib, the station manager, did not let anyone leave, fearing that there may be violence. The riot police came to escort us out of the building safely. The only incident that happened was that someone threw a Coca-Cola bottle and almost hit one of the employees while chanting, "Go away American devils."

When I arrived the next day, there were still a few protestors, but they were generally peaceful. The only disruption was them chanting loudly as each person walked into the building.

We kept broadcasting our controversial topics, until the demonstrators realized that we were not going anywhere. In fact, within a month, we had one of the most popular broadcasts in UAE, and some of the surrounding countries. It actually started a movement for equal rights in education in countries where women were traditionally excluded from attending school.

The United Nations addressed some of these issues with fervor, and their first step was to impose sanctions against countries within the Union that did not enforce a woman's right to education. It was a big win as far as we were concerned. We were recognized as the station taking on the fight against inequality in the Arabic and Muslim communities, and I was nominated for a Nobel Peace Prize Award for my worldwide voice on this issue.

I had only been working in this area for a few months, but due to luck or otherwise, big changes happened. I knew that it may have happened without me, but I was excited to be in the right place at the right time. And although I did not win the Nobel Peace Prize, I felt privileged to have been considered for such a prestigious accolade.

I enjoyed Dubai and all of its frills. I learned how to ski at Ski Dubai, which was the first indoor ski resort, located in the Mall of the Emirates. I partook in everything from sandboarding in the dessert to dining at the Top of the World. I really enjoyed the indoor Disneyworld-like amusement park, IMG Worlds of Adventure.

But after about five months, I was homesick. I missed everything from giving sloppy kisses to Sly, to eating a piece of Frenchy's fried chicken. One night after leaving the station, I decided that I wanted to go out, instead of going home. Home was a lonely place these days. In Houston, I was so accustomed to always having someone around. Even when Auntie Char started spending more time with Roni, I found myself staying with Sweezy, Sly, and their staff.

I heard about this spot where a lot of Europeans and Americans hung out. I walked in and there was a live band playing, "Joy and Pain." I immediately knew that I was in the right place. I sat at the bar between a white woman and a black man. The lady spoke right away, while the man acted as if I did not exist. The bartender came over and asked what was I drinking, and I told him a lemon drop, made with U'luvka. I thought Grey Goose was good vodka, until I tasted U'luvka, which was Polish vodka, and became my drink of choice when not drinking wine.

I was enjoying the band, bopping my head, and demolishing my fourth lemon drop when a short, little white American guy, dressed in very colorful clothing came and asked me if I wanted to dance. Before answering, I looked him up and down, which was not that much of a distance, but thought, what the hell. I had not danced in a while, so who cared if I looked like a giraffe dancing with a flamingo.

We danced to about three songs until the band played Kem's, *I Can't Stop Loving You.* I don't know if it was the music, being away from family, or the drinks, more than likely it was a combination of all of that, I broke down crying on the dance floor. My dance partner said, "I am sorry, I did not mean for my dancing to cause you to cry."

I laughed and said, "No, it is not you. Thank you for the dance."

I ran out of the club and called my driver who told me that he was in the vicinity. He pulled up about five minutes later and asked, "So where would you like to go now, Ms. DuBois?"

"I am ready to go home, Eman. Thank you."

While riding home, a sadness engulfed my entire being. I had a silent conversation with God. *Lord, I thought I was following my destiny and that you had ordained my mission to help others. But in doing so, I am feeling as if something is missing from my life. I love you Lord, and want to fulfill whatever I am supposed to do in your name. I want my life to be committed to a cause. However, if I am misdirected, please give me a sign.*

When I arrived home, the house was cold and empty. I took a shower, crawled into my bed, and cried. I cried myself to sleep, and was awaken by the ringing of my phone. It was Sweezy and Sly calling to check on me. Sweezy said Sly had been begging to call me for two days, so he knew that he had to call. We talked for hours before finally hanging up.

I felt a lot better just hearing from them. Sly had started playing the guitar and actually played me a song on the phone. I had to admit, without any bias, for a beginner, he was quite talented. I dozed back off to sleep after speaking with them. The next time I woke up, I was in a cold sweat. I had a dream that I was running away from a man on a horse, swinging a lasso, trying to rope me as if I were livestock.

Chapter 28

Chief came to visit Dubai during my sixth month there. We went out to dinner and he asked me how things were going. I told him that things could not be better. He looked me directly in my eyes and said, "My spirit is telling me something different. Do you care to discuss it?" I admitted to Chief that I was battling with a bout of loneliness. I missed my family in Houston. He insisted that I take some time off to visit them.

He said he knew from personal experience, that it is difficult being alone in a foreign country. According to Chief, when he was younger, he took a job promotion where he was assigned to China. He said he had a very difficult time adjusting to the culture there, and being by himself. Chief said he quit the job within two months of being relocated to China, but the company refused to pay his way back to the U.S. He struggled in China for another two months until he got enough money to return.

I asked Chief what were the plans for the broadcast after the year in Dubai. He informed me that the lawyers were negotiating a deal to broadcast from the States with UAE state officials. He said that they were in the final stages, and should be signing a deal soon. He also told me that it would have to be a different format than how we currently simulcast, but it would probably only add a few more hours to my workday.

After I looked at him strangely, he told me that he did not want to bore me with all the intricate details, but I would have to work with two different programming mangers. I told Chief I would like to hear all of the details once the deal was finalized.

He told me he would make certain that happened but also told me that the only way we would succeed at international syndication, is if I was willing to take on the assignment. He recognized that other people could do the job, but he did not think anyone could replace my flair, personality, or passion. I thought that it was odd that he classified my honest and brutal opinion as flair and personality.

After speaking with Chief, I felt a little relieved knowing that I would not be in Dubai indefinitely. I was completely spoiled by being catered to all of the time, but I was willing to give it all up just to see my Snug Bug smile and say, "Hi Teepee."

I had spoken with Penny a few times because she said she needed an intervention as it related to Ty. From listening to her conversation, Ty was being a little overprotective. I think once he found out that Penny had her period, he was scared of the possibility of her becoming a teenage mother. He insisted that she could not go anywhere without adult supervision. I was able to talk her through a way to resolve her conflict with Ty on several occasions.

Penny was definitely morphing into a typical teenage girl, and it was also clear to me that Ty was having a difficult time with her transformation. I also missed Ty. I missed him calling me Pocahontas, telling me how beautiful I was, and how he would never give up on us. It seemed like those days were far behind us now. I purposely did not ask Penny any personal questions about Ty. I knew that many women, and probably some men, chased after him; but I wondered whether he had found anyone that he was genuinely interested in being with.

The day I packed for my trip to Houston, I was very lively and upbeat. I knew that I had a long trip ahead, but I could not wait until I landed. I decided to surprise everyone and not let them know that I was coming.

When I arrived at IAH, it was strange to catch a taxi back to the house. When I arrived home, there was no one there. Roni decided to give up her apartment to move in with Auntie Char. I was surprised to see all new furniture in the living room and one of the walls had been knocked down, which actually made the living room look much larger. I journeyed into the kitchen and I saw that all of the cabinets had been replaced, and there were all new appliances.

Auntie Char asked me whether I mind if they did some updates, but I had not expected to see such drastic changes so fast. Roni was a carpenter by trade, and it was evident that she was using her skills to update Aunt Hattie's house.

I went into my room, and it was the same as it had been for years. I felt so comfortable just falling down on my bed; although the mattress was probably almost thirty years old, lumpy, and springs hit my back if I laid on the wrong side. However, just the familiarity of being in a place that I called home, made me feel like I was lying in a queen's bed in a castle.

I ventured into Aunt Hattie's room, which also had not been changed since her death. I looked around and smiled thinking about the argument Mystery and I had long ago when she wanted to get rid of all of Aunt Hattie's possessions, and redecorate the room. Who knew one day that I would be living with only memories of the both of them? I could never find the words that could accurately verbalize how much I missed them.

I was trying to fight off my tears when Roni entered into the room holding a gun and said, "Hi, Porchia. Girl, I got my gat cuz I thought we had a break-in. What are you doing here?"

"I live here, remember," I said smiling walking toward to give her a hug, but hesitant of the gun she was holding.

She must have read my mind, because she quickly put the gun in her waistband, hugged me, then said, "This is a surprise. I was trying to have the kitchen and the bathroom done before you returned. How was Dubai?"

"It's great. But I missed y'all."

"We missed you too! Chardonnay has been walking around pouting ever since you left."

"Yeah, yeah, so you say, but I am certain you have given her many reasons to smile."

"I try to, but it does not seem I can quite compete with her niece that she adores."

"Oh, yeah," I chuckled. "So where is my aunt?" I asked.

"At work as usual. So are you back for good?"

"No, just for a short visit. I was homesick and the big boss came to Dubai and insisted that I get away."

"Well, it is good to see you. I came back to do some measurements for the kitchen. I am buying some slate for the counter, and wood for the floor."

"Wow, sounds nice. I can't wait to see your final product."

"Me too. It would be great to get your input while you're here," Roni said.

"No, do your thang. I am easy. Plus, my idea of a home improvement is buying a new pillow for the sofa."

Roni laughed and said, "Okay, well, let me get back to work. Again, glad that you are back."

I hugged her again. "Thanks, Roni."

I still felt that I had not gotten the opportunity to get to know Roni. After coming back from Puerto Vallarta, I was busily preparing for my trip to Dubai. But he seemed to be a really cool person. Thinking about Roni made me think about my other younger brothers and sisters. I felt bad that I had not been able to spend much time with them either. I decided to make a date night for all of us, including Sly, to hang out.

Although I'd had no contact with my younger siblings since I left for Dubai, I had spoken to Tracy several times. She seemed to be enjoying life with Javier. However, Tracy had not spoken much to her family since she moved to Las Vegas. I knew her mother, Ms. Carletta, was not pleased about Tracy moving in with a man and not being married. But, Tracy told me that she was ready to live her life, without caring about what others thought.

According to Tracy, when she was young, she spent most of her time raising her brothers and sisters, and sexually pleasing her father. When I think about that child molesting man, it makes me sick to the stomach. I felt good that Tracy seemed to be finally adjusting to what that man did to her, but the other part of me was disappointed that she was so distant from her family.

After getting settled into my room, I decided to surprise Sweezy and Sly. When I arrived, only Ms. Marvelle was around. "Where is everyone?" I asked.

"Well, Sweezy gave Ausprey some time off, so she is visiting her family in New Jersey. And Sweezy and Master Sly are at football practice. He's quite a player, you know."

"Really, he's good?"

"Yes, he is the one that runs with the ball. He is a quick one, you know."

"So how long have they been gone?"

"Uh, 'bout fifteen minutes or so," Ms. Marvelle said as if she really was not certain.

"Do you think I can catch them at practice?"

"Yes, I don't know why not. They are usually gone for hours."

Ms. Marvelle gave me directions to the playing field. One thing I realized was I did not miss driving around the city. Houston's traffic was crazy, it could take anywhere from thirty minutes to an hour, even when going only ten minutes away.

When I arrived, I saw Sweezy out on the field yelling at the boys as if they were practicing for a NFL game. I then saw Snug Bug lining up in the backfield. The play was designed for him, and once he received the ball, he looked like lightening running and swerving up the field. I started screaming and shouting, which caused Sweezy to look back. Once Sweezy recognized it was me, he stopped what he was doing to run over to me.

"What the hell are you doing here, Swoosh?" he asked while hugging me tightly.

Before I could answer, Sly had run over and was pulling on my leg, shouting, "Teepee! Teepee!"

The practice came to a complete stop because we were quite a spectacle to observe.

"Hi, guys, I am happy to see you too, but I did not mean to interrupt practice."

"Yelling like a crazy woman and you did not mean to interrupt?" Sweezy laughed. He looked at one of the other parents and told him to continue with practice.

Then he looked at Sly and said, "You go back out there too. Teepee will be here when practice is over."

"No, Dad, if you are not coaching, why do I have to go out there and play?"

Sweezy gave him the look and he marched back out on the field.

Sweezy led me to the bench and pretty much made me sit and asked, "Is there something wrong?"

"No, I just missed you all. I needed to get away."

"We have missed you too. But is the job going okay?"

"Yes, everything is fine, Pops," I said while grabbing his hand.

He smiled and said, "Well, you are a sight for sore eyes!"

Chapter 29

I spent the evening catching up with Sweezy and Sly after practice. Sly was in a very inquisitive state of mind. He asked me a lot about where I lived, what did I do there, and when I was coming back. Then he shocked me, and started talking about Mystery and wanted to know things about his grandparents.

That's when I realized that there was a whole part of my history that I knew nothing about. I did not have anyone to talk to about it, because both Mystery and Aunt Hattie were gone. I am not certain I wanted to know about my child abusing father's side of the family, but at that point, it is not just something interesting to know, but it could affect us if we have any health issues. I had to wonder, *did we have any hereditary diseases or dysfunctions that ran in our family?*

When I returned home, Auntie Char and Roni were opening the box of a brand new 65-inch television. Auntie Char looked up and when she saw me she yelled, "My baby is home!"

"Hi, Auntie Char," I said smiling. "I guess you missed me."

"You don't know how much, girl, come here and give me some love!"

I walked over and gave her a hug."

"Look at you, you have gained some weight on your scrawny body."

I laughed and said, "I was never scrawny, Auntie."

"Yeah, but you're getting butt and hips, looking like your mother."

"Speaking of my mother, when you are done, do you mind me picking your brain about a few things?"

"Hey, I can take care of this. Why don't you two take some time to talk," said Roni.

"Ah, you are such a sweetie, love, but are you sure you can handle it alone?"

"Well, I did not want to say anything, but you are all up in my grill just putting salt in my game love," said Roni.

Chardonnay playfully shoved Roni and said, "Whateva buddah!" Then she looked at me and said, "Come on Porchia, let's go to Starbucks and give Roni a chance to realize how much she really needs me."

We drove to Starbucks, but it was closed. Chardonnay suggested going to a little diner that she knew stayed open twenty-four hours.

We got there and snuggled into a booth. The waitress came right away to ask us what she could get us. Auntie Char ordered a fish sandwich and a Pepsi and I ordered a sweet tea. After the waitress left, Auntie Char asked me, "So what's up, baby?"

"I need your help in filling in some of my gaps."

"Gaps about what?"

"Anything you knew about your mother and grandmother."

"Wow, I did not expect that."

"So what do you know?"

"Really, I know only what my father and Mystery told me. I have a lot of missing information too."

"Auntie Char, I know that you don't have it all, but anything that you have would be greatly appreciated."

"Okay, I might need something stronger than Pepsi for this talk."

Auntie Char gestured for the waitress to come over and she said, "Can you change that Pepsi to wine?"

"What type of wine? We have Merlot, Chardonnay, or Moscato," responded the waitress.

"Bring me a glass of Moscato, please."

"Okay, your drinks will be right up."

"Sorry Porchia, but I need a drink. I still get upset when I think about my grandmother." Auntie Char said.

"Why?" I asked.

"Okay, let me start with the way I have been told the story. My grandmother, your great grandmother, ran a ho house. According to my dad, she only cared about money. She treated her own daughter, your grandmother, very badly. She used her to make money, along with a lot of other women."

"She pimped out her own daughter?" I asked.

The waitress came over with our drinks and Auntie Char told the waitress to bring her another one with her meal. Auntie Char took the drink and pretty much downed it in two gulps. She then said, "Yes, she pimped out our mother when she was like eight or nine years old. To her, our mother was nothing but a commodity. If she did not bring in money, she was no good to her. Well, my father met your grandmother when she was fifteen and fell in love with her. He met her at the ho house your great grandmother ran.

"At a ho house?" I asked with a frown on my face.

"Yes, and according to him, although she was a prostitute, she was a beautiful innocent, naïve young lady that needed love and nurturing. After spending a few times with her, he decided that he wanted her all for himself."

"Wasn't he already married?" I asked.

"Yeah, but he said he no longer loved his wife, and he was willing to leave his wife for a chance at a life with your grandmother. Well, your great grandmother heard about his plans and had him beaten very badly and threatened to kill him if he ever had contact with her again."

"But he did have contact afterward with her, right?"

"No, but shortly after cutting her ties with him, your grandmother found out that she was pregnant with his baby. This is where the story gets crazy. Your great grandmother was going to make your grandmother abort the baby, and that baby was me. Well, your grandmother, my mother, tried to get in touch with my father, but instead found his wife, the lady I thought was my mother most of my life."

"I am confused," I said.

"Just bear with me. So the wife convinced your grandmother, my mother, to run away. The wife found a place for your grandmother to keep her away from her mother, who wanted to abort the baby because while pregnant, your grandmother could not make money for your great grandmother. Well, the wife told your grandmother, if she would just have the baby, she would take care of her and the baby. But, the only way she would do this is, if she did not tell her husband that she was pregnant. So the wife kept your grandmother in hiding for the entire pregnancy. She fed her, clothed her, and housed her."

The waitress came over with Auntie Char's fish sandwich and another glass of wine. The waitress looked and said, 'May I get you anything else?"

Chardonnay looked at her and said, "Just another glass of Moscato, the check, and after that, some privacy, please."

"I will get that to you right away," said the waitress.

"Thanks," replied Auntie Char.

Auntie Char took another big gulp of her wine and said, "Where was I at?"

"Why did the woman who raised you take care of my grandmother during pregnancy?" I asked.

"So this was the deal. Her husband was about to leave her, so she needed to act as if she was pregnant. She got things to make her stomach look big and everything. She told her husband, my dad, that they could not have sex during pregnancy because it might endanger the child. The wife had already attempted to have three babies with her husband, but she was never able to bring them to term. The husband desperately wanted a child, so he believed everything that she said. And he definitely did not want do anything to cause harm to his baby."

"So he never saw her naked or anything? I am not certain how she pulled that one off." I said.

"Well, she did. She ended up having a 'baby' at home while he was away on a business trip. He came back and had a precious little baby girl, me, which he loved and adored. She told him that she went into labor and called a midwife to deliver the baby at the house. And my mother, your grandmother, went along with the plan because she was able to save my life, and have me raised by my father."

"So my great grandmother did not know where my grandmother was hiding? That seems weird since The Ward is so small, and she supposedly had a lot of connections."

"No, your great grandmother eventually found out and figured a way to make a profit out of it. She made the woman who raised me pay her five thousand dollars for me. She collected the money, and told your grandmother that was the price she had to pay for her freedom. Your grandmother never went back to her mother's house, but had to return to prostituting as a means of survival."

"And your dad never knew that his wife was not the mother of his child."

Auntie Char was on her third glass of wine, so she was speaking a little slower. She said, "He found out when I was six months old that she had bought the baby. But my mom never told him that she had bought the baby from his ex-lover, nor did he know that he was my biological father. He only found out after my mom died. She confessed everything to me, so I tracked my father down to let him know that he had a biological daughter."

"My great grandmother seemed to be straight from the devil. She was an evil woman."

"Well, her name was fitting, Eva DuBois. Do you know your grandmother's name?"

"I don't remember. I believe Mystery may have told me once."

"Her name was Prosperity DuBois," said Auntie Char.

"So that is the DuBois Curse that Mystery was trying to protect me from?"

"Yes, Mystery really felt the DuBois women were cursed to be hoes. She was so glad that Sly was born a male. She figured the DuBois Curse ended with you."

"Well, she would be glad to know that I might be cursed to be a nun," I said laughing.

"She would be proud of you, regardless. She just thought it was her duty to make certain you had some other opportunities given to you outside of prostituting."

"Auntie Char, how did you feel about it after you found out?"

"I was angry. I did some horrible things to Mystery as a result of my anger. I felt as if she was given the opportunities that I never had."

"But you know she was raped at an early age and saw her mother overdose on drugs."

"Yeah, but you know, Porchia, as the old folks used to say, the grass always seems greener on the other side of the fence. With time and the Lord, I learned how to positively channel my anger. That is when I think I reached out to Mystery, but she still did not believe me. I am just glad I had the opportunity to attempt to make up for evil things that I did to her, and that she forgave me."

"Wow, Auntie Char, I am not quite sure what to say about our family. It seems like the only thing that may have ran in our family was ho'in. I think I may be able to deal with that," I said and laughed.

"Girl, that ho'in gene ain't nuttin' to play with. That is why I got married," retorted Auntie Char.

"Well, I really appreciate you reliving some hard memories. It just seemed like a part of me was missing."

"Anytime and anything for my adorable niece."

Chapter 30

I left Houston feeling that I had completed a mission, but I still felt empty inside. I realized that everyone had a support system, including my younger sisters and brothers, which would keep them going in my absence.

However, I am not certain that I had a support system adequate to help me get through my time in Dubai. I could hear Aunt Hattie telling me, "It is okay to let someone take care of you Baby Girl."

The truth of the matter was, I did not trust anyone to take care of me the way that God took care of me, or the way I felt that I could take care of myself. There were times that I miss the presence of a physical being, and leaving Houston magnified my feeling of loneliness.

When I arrived back at the station, everyone was happy to see me. I was working with such intensity that Habib pulled me aside and told me I needed to ease up a little. I knew that I had another tough six months ahead of me, but all I could think about was returning home.

However, within a few weeks of being back, I settled into my regular work routine, and did not have time to miss home. We were increasing listeners by two hundred percent on a weekly basis. There was a drop in listeners over the two-week period I spent in Houston, but to my surprise, we quickly surpassed all projected goals for the quarter.

I received a phone call in the middle of the night and the caller said, "Go back home, devil," with an Arabic accent. This was the first time I received a call as such, on my personal line, so I became a little concerned. I went back to sleep realizing that it was probably just another scare tactic by some radical group.

I received another call at 3:00 a.m. from Habib telling me that the station had been burnt to the ground. He informed me that all broadcasting would be suspended until further notice. While speaking with Habib, Abbas called, so I asked Habib please keep me informed. Abbas told me that we received a threat from a Muslim extremist group that said if we continued with our Western views and topics, we all would be subject to death.

Everyone seemed to be a little concerned, but I became angry and wanted to continue broadcasting some way. I called Larry at the corporate office, and he said he was about to call me. He told me they received credible information that this extremist group was planning kidnappings, and promising decapitation of Americans on live t.v. As a result of this treat, the company was arranging transport of the station's employees out of Dubai.

I asked Larry if we would be going to a place where it would be safe to broadcast. Larry informed me that we were going to temporarily suspend all broadcasting from the Middle East.

My belief was that we should not allow small groups of people to dictate policy as it relates to issues pertaining to the masses. It was evident that people in Arabic countries were ready for change, but because we were being threatened; we were ready and willing to give up on our cause. I received several calls from other employees, everybody seemed to be nervous and ready to abandon what we had achieved within the short time we had been in Dubai.

Corporate wanted me to leave right away, but I talked them into letting me stay until the end of the week. I did not want extreme groups to make me run. Additionally, there were a few things that I wanted to get from Dubai, prior to going home. I did not get an opportunity to visit the Souks, so I wanted to ensure that I shopped before returning to Houston. Sweezy requested a cartouche, and I wanted to make sure one was handcrafted for both him and Sly. I also had to visit the spice souk to pick up some spices for Auntie Char. And I was not going to pass on my opportunity to get some of Dubai's artwork.

After a long day of shopping with a bodyguard at my side, I wanted to escape to the comfort of my place without feeling as if I could not take a step without someone watching. I was provided guards at my place as well, but at least they were outside, instead of in my personal space.

When my driver and my bodyguard took me back to my house, I could see that there were people standing in front of my door. I jumped out to see what was going on. To my amazement, Ty was standing talking to some of the security.

"Ty, what are you doing here?" I asked.

"I heard about what was going on here on the news. I wanted to come to make certain you were okay."

"Ty, why didn't you just call?"

"I was taking no chances. If something happened to you, I would not forgive myself."

I just shook my head in amazement and said, "Come on, let's go in the house."

My bodyguard that had been following me all day asked, "Ms. DuBois, are you going to be okay?"

"Yes, I will. Thanks for the escort."

"You are welcome, Ms. DuBois. There will be at least two people here with you all night."

"Thank you, goodnight."

"Goodnight Ms. DuBois."

When I closed the door Ty said, "I think he has a crush on you."

"Ty, the man is just doing his job."

"No, I can tell by the way he was looking at you."

"And so what if he does?"

"I just think you needed to be aware."

"So back to why you are here Ty."

"To get you back home safely."

"And you thought I was incapable of doing that alone?" I asked.

"Yes, I mean no, I don't know what I mean. It was just scary hearing information come across saying that all Americans were in jeopardy. I just wanted to make certain I was here to escort you home safely."

"So now you are my personal security?"

"Pocahontas, why are you being so hard on me?" "Because, you could be putting your life in jeopardy! We both don't need to be in danger."

"I won't let anything happen. My job is to get you back to Houston safely."

"Well, I guess it's too late. What is done is already done."

"So, is it okay for me to stay with you?" Ty asked.

"Where else would you stay?"

"I could find a hotel, but I would feel better if I could be close to you."

"Humn, I should punish you and send you to a hotel, but it is okay if you stay here. I have extra rooms."

"Cool, I am going out to ask my driver to bring in my bags. Be right back."

"I don't think that special forces outside would let me go anywhere even if I tried."

Ty said, "Well, good, I am glad that they agree with me on that."

My chef was gone for the evening, so I went to the kitchen to see if I could prepare something for Ty to eat. My chef did most of the grocery shopping, so I did not know what was available. I found some frozen chicken breasts, so I started defrosting them.

When Ty walked back in, I asked him if he was hungry, and he told me that he was starving. I knew I had Swiss cheese and ham, so I decided that I would cook Chicken Cordon Bleu.

Ty looked surprised and said, "Are you going to try to cook?"

"See, there's a lot you need to know about me. I know how to cook, dude. What else would you expect with Aunt Hattie as my inspiration?"

"Well, I don't know if you can touch Aunt Hattie's cooking. But I do know that you're full of surprises. And believe me, I ain't complaining."

I had dinner made within the hour. Ty demolished the chicken, green beans, and rice pilaf. He usually took his time and had conversation during his meals, but the only thing that came out of his mouth was, "Dang, Pocahontas, this is slammin'."

I felt good knowing that he enjoyed my cooking. As we started discussing what he wanted to do while we were still in Dubai, my phone rang.

"Hi, Porchia, have you seen the news?"

"No Abbas, what's up?"

"All flights from Dubai, back and forth to the U.S., have been temporarily suspended. There have been threats against the airlines, so we are on high security alert."

"So, we won't be able to get out?" I asked.

"No, I don't think any time soon. Additionally, they want to put us all in a hotel on high security alert with twenty-four hour protection."

"I have security now at my house. I think I am safe here," I said.

"Well, we are short on security, so therefore, we have chosen to put people in the same place so no one will be without protection."

"When do we need to leave for the hotel?" I asked

"Tomorrow morning."

"Okay, Abbas, thanks for calling."

"See you tomorrow."

When I hung up the phone Ty said, "What was that about?"

"We probably won't be able to leave on Friday."

"What's up?"

"All flights to and from the U.S. has been suspended because of threats to the airlines."

"What!"

"See, that is why I did not want you to come. We both don't need to be in danger. You did not consider what would happen to Penny if something happened to you."

"If something happened to you, life would be unbearable for me."

"And if something happened to you, life would be unbearable for Penny."

"Pocahontas, I'm not certain why we're having this discussion. Nothing will happen to either one of us."

"Let's pray not."

Chapter 31

We were all sequestered to a hotel that had all of the amenities that we could possibly want, including restaurants, spa, boutiques, and entertainment. The hotel guests were primarily Americans, or those closely associated with Americans. Everyone from the station was there, even some that were citizens of Dubai, because the extremist group supposedly had placed them on a target list.

Ty and I shared a two-bedroom suite because he insisted on being my protector. I had to admit, I felt more secure with him being so close. We spent our days playing board games, talking and laughing, and spent our nights watching American classics like *The Cosby Show,* *The Parkers,* and *Girlfriends.*

One afternoon, Ty decided that he wanted to do some shopping and asked me whether I cared to join him; I told him I would pass, because I was working on some broadcasting ideas to continue our broadcast in the region. Shortly after Ty left, I heard a big boom that shook the room, followed by alarms. I ran to the hall and saw people scrambling all about. They were screaming that the elevators had stopped and the exit doors on the floor were locked.

I ran back into my room and attempted to dial the front desk to see what was going on. The phone rang, but there was no answer. I called Ty's phone, and there was no answer. I started worrying about Ty, so I ran back into the hallway to see if anyone had any information.

An American man said that there was an explosion on the ground floor, and a lot of people were injured. I went into the room to see if the television worked and whether there was anything being broadcast. Surprisingly, BBC was already broadcasting that there was total destruction at the hotel. People were being hauled off in ambulances, while others were laid out dead in front of the cameras. I changed the channel to CNN, and they were reporting that a suicide bomber had driven a van into the ground floor of the hotel.

I tried calling Ty's number again and did not get an answer. I looked at my phone and Chief was calling, so I answered.

"Hey, Porchia, I am just checking on you. I heard your hotel was targeted by terrorists."

"I am not sure what is going on, but my friend came here and now he is missing. I am stuck on this floor and can't get any information! I can't even get the reception desk!"

"Okay, Porchia, calm down. Let me see what I can find out. What is his name?"

"Tyrese Gamble."

"The basketball player?"

"Yes, that's him."

"Okay, I'm on it!"

It hit me like a strike of lightening that I may have lost Ty forever. I went into the hallway and started pushing on the doors to see if I could open them. One of the engineers from the station saw me shoving the door and ran toward me and said, "Ms. DuBois, are you all right?"

I screamed, "No, I am not all right. Ty may be down there injured and I need to get to him. He needs me now."

"Ms. DuBois, I don't think we will get down there soon. It is chaotic and they are trying to take care of injured people. The best thing you can do is go to your room and wait for further instructions."

Then I heard a bang and the door opened. It was hotel staff checking on us to see if we were okay. They told us that it seems that all of the floors are okay with the exception of the ground floor and the garage. They said that they would have further instructions on what to do on the hotel's television station. Until then, we should return to our rooms.

It was unbearable waiting on information on Ty. I would never forgive myself if something happened to him. Once I found Ty, I won't waste another minute, another second, without telling him how I really felt about him.

God, just give me that chance. Lord you have given me the ability to love and forgive. I need the ability to trust Ty again. I believe that we have a chance at happiness. I have lost too many people in my lifetime. I could not stand to lose another person. Especially one that I love and have pushed away, time after time. If it is your will, I want for me, Ty and Penny to have a life together. Lord please give me the ability to know that I can love myself enough for a chance at happiness with Ty. Lord, please give me the courage to trust that you will lead and direct my heart in the way it should go. I ask this in your darling son's Jesus' name, Amen.

I prayed and prayed for me to be able to see Ty just once again. The hotel phone rang and I picked it up.

"Hi, Porchia, this is Chief. I have been trying to call you and your cell phone is not working."

"Any news, Chief?" I asked.

He told me that he was sorry, but that they had accounted for all of the people at the hotel who were in the hospital. Ty must have been one of the bodies that they had been attempting to recover underneath the rubble. According to Chief, first responders did not believe that anyone had survived the blast. I went completely silent on the phone. Chief called my name several times and I could not answer. When I was able to put my words together I said, "Chief, you have to be wrong. Ty's not dead!"

I heard a knock on my door, I ran to the door thinking it had to be Ty. But it was only the hotel staff delivering food to our floor. I told them I was not hungry and asked about the recovery effort. One of the employees told me that it probably would be morning before it would be safe for us to leave the hotel. I asked the hotel worker whether we would be briefed, and he said they were still trying to figure out things.

After about thirty minutes of me sitting in a stupor watching different broadcast about the events going on around me, I heard a knock on the door. I ran to the door and said, "Ty, I knew you were okay!"

When I opened the door, it was Habib. Habib looked at me sadly. "Sorry, Porchia, I understand that your friend has been declared dead. They found a man that met his description. The body is badly charred, so it will be difficult to make a positive identification. They will do some additional examination to positively determine whether it is him. In the meantime, we are being moved to another location. They are trying to make certain that the security measures are in place so we won't have a repeat. I was informed that you should be back in the United States in about two days."

I heard what Habib was saying, but it was like he was speaking Japanese. I could not go back home without Ty. I could not tell Penny that she had lost another person. I could not live the rest of my life without Ty. How could God allow this to happen to us?

During my phone call with Chief, I asked him to call my family and let them know how they could get in touch with me. By the time Sweezy called, I had an emotional break down and could not talk. I told him I was okay, and would call him later. A little later Auntie Char called, and all I could do is cry. I had no words. I was completely engulfed with sadness. I hung up the phone with Auntie Char and told her I would call her back soon.

I made up my mind; I was not going to leave Dubai until I saw Ty. I was told that his body was unidentifiable, but I could not accept that Ty was gone forever. I could not accept that I would not have the opportunity to let him know how I really felt about him. I did not get a chance to say bye to Chanti. I did not get an opportunity to say bye to Aunt Hattie. And now, I am being denied the opportunity to say bye to Ty.

I asked Habib to use his contacts to get me in to see Ty. Habib worked it out and I was escorted to the place where they were holding unidentified bodies. When I saw Ty's body lying there on the metal slab, my knees got weak.

I screamed, "No, Ty, you can't be gone! We had an entire life ahead of us!" I don't know what happened after that because I woke up in what seemed to be a hospital room with an IV in my arm.

I rang the call button and an Indian woman came in and said, "Oh, you are finally awake."

"What am I doing here?" I asked.

"You blacked out and were unresponsive. You were rushed to the hospital by ambulance."

"What's wrong with me? I don't remember any of that."

"We think it was just fatigue, exhaustion and lack of food and water. Do you remember the last time you ate?"

"No, but I need to get home. I have a lot to take care of. I have not spoken to my family. They must be worried. Chief said my phone was not working. "

"Well, we need you to get your strength back before you will be able to take a flight to the U.S."

"Is there a doctor I can speak with?"

No, there was another explosion at a western hotel. The doctors are all attending to injured people."

"Were there more fatalities?"

"Yes, this one brought down the entire building."

"What is going on? Do they know who is responsible?"

"Yes, the group has come forward and claimed responsibility. U.S. troops are being deployed here as we speak."

"Would I be able to return home if I was not sick?" "

"Yes, there have been several emergency evacuations. People are leaving in military aircraft. And my job is to get you healthy so you can go soon too.

"I can't leave Ty. I would like for him to be transported back when I leave to go to U.S."

"I am sorry. Who is Ty?"

"The one and only man that I have ever loved. He was killed in the first bombing. I am not leaving without him!"

"Oh, I am so sorry to hear that. But you should get your rest, and we will figure out everything later."

Chapter 32

I stayed in the hospital for two days after being initially admitted. Chief called frequently to check on my condition, and he told me he would attempt to expedite my release. Chief also got in touch with Sweezy to let him know that I would be home soon.

Habib made certain the he also visited frequently during my stay. I found it odd that Abbas had not attempted to contact me. I asked Habib about Abbas, and he held his head down for a while before speaking. He finally looked at me and said, "We lost Abbas in the first blast."

"Why did you not tell me this before?"

"You had enough to worry about with your friend."

"What does this group want?" I asked.

"They want us to leave and not broadcast anymore."

"Habib, we can't let them win. We need to find a way to stay and broadcast."

"Sorry, Porchia, the government will not allow it. Dubai has always separated themselves from the rest of the Muslim world. We are in a full-fledged war right now."

"So does that mean people's voices should be silenced? I would hate to think Ty and Abbas died for nothing."

"I think we have made a difference. After the war, we will see changes, and you had a lot to do with it," he said.

"I pray that one day I will be able to see it like you do. I see failure. I see that we have lost lives of people that were very special to us. Ty had nothing to do with anything going on here; yet, he is dead and we don't see change. We see additional violence. Who knows how this will all end?"

I was released to another hotel, where supposedly the security was extremely tight because high-ranking U.S. military officials were also staying at this hotel. No one could come in or leave without proper identification. Everyone was on rotation to leave Dubai to go back to the U.S. They still were not allowing commercial jets to fly in and out of Dubai. My day finally came for me to return back home.

Sweezy was extremely worried about me, and my mental state, so he attempted to get permission to escort me back to the U.S.; however, the American government denied his request. They defended their position by saying it was a war state, and not safe for Americans to travel to the area. All of the military efforts were designed to fight the extremists, not protect U.S. citizens.

I was packing to get ready for my flight, the next day, when I received a call from the reception desk informing me that they needed to speak with me. I asked the lady on the phone what required me to go to the desk to handle. She responded, "I will have to let you speak to the manager so he can explain more."

"That's okay, in order to save us both time, I am on my way," I told her.

I walked down to the desk, and I saw this tall, black guy standing at the desk. I looked at the front desk attendant and said, "Hi, someone called me and asked me to come down."

"Are you, Ms. DuBois?" asked the attendant.

"Yes, I am."

The man standing within an earshot said, "Hello, Ms. DuBois, I need to speak with you."

I must have had a strange look on my face because the man started speaking fast and said, "I am with the Central Intelligence Agency, and I just need a moment of your time. The hotel has arranged a private room for us to have a discussion. Please follow me."

We exited the elevator once we got to the twenty-fourth floor. The man did not say another word until we approached the door. At that time he said, "Ms. DuBois, I have some people that need to speak with you."

He opened the door and there were about five other dark suits in the room that was converted into an office. I really started worrying that something was seriously wrong, but could not figure out how I was involved. There was a big burly guy, who reminded me of pictures that I had seen of J. Edgar Hoover, who got up from behind the desk, extended his hands and said, "Thank you Ms. DuBois for agreeing to meet us. My name is Richard Sherman."

The other men who were sitting in chairs, which were strategically positioned around the room, directly facing the burly man at the big desk, also stood.

I reluctantly shook his hand and said, "Mr. Sherman, with all due respect sir, I did not agree to meet with anyone. I was escorted here with no explanation. I would appreciate knowing what is going on."

"Ms. DuBois, please have a seat," the burly man said as he pointed to a chair in front of his desk and as on cue, all of the other men in the black suits sat.

Once I sat he said, "There is nothing for you to worry about. We are here to tell you that we are proud of what you have attempted to do in this part of the world. As you know, the United States has been fighting this battle with ISIS, ISIL, QJBR, and other terrorists groups in this region for a while now. We are sorry that we were not able to provide you with the security you needed. But we thought our presence in Dubai would cause a media flurry, and be counterproductive to what we have been trying to accomplish here."

"Sir, I am sorry, but I don't understand what any of this has to do with me."

"We have been working with the government here to help combat terrorism for a while. The group that is behind the bombings specifically targeted your friend,

Tyrese Gamble. He was captured by this notorious group, and was being held captive."

"Sir, no disrespect, but what are you talking about? I saw Ty on a slab!"

"Yes, Ms. DuBois. That was a decoy because we could not let the media know that Ty Gamble had been captured by terrorists. We could not risk the years that we had invested in our mission, nor risk a chance at putting the entire world in jeopardy. I know that this may not make any sense to you Ms. DuBois, but this is a very sensitive and highly confidential campaign that we have been operating. We knew that the terrorists would not cause any harm to Mr. Gamble. We had something that they wanted badly, and if something happened to Mr. Gamble, they definitely would not have gotten it."

"So wait, are you telling me that Ty is alive?" I asked.

"Yes, ma'am."

"Oh my God! That is excellent news! Is he okay?"

"Yes, he is being debriefed. But he is in good health."

"Can I see him?"

"No, he will be going to D.C. to speak with some of our people there after we finish our debriefing here."

"I am not going to leave without seeing him sir."

"We will arrange for you to meet him in D.C."

"When will that be?"

"We will escort you to D.C. on a private military jet that leaves in two hours."

"I am ready, but when will I see Ty?"

"You should be able to see him within a few days."

"I will need to contact my family and let them know that I am okay and will be going to D.C. for a few days."

"No Ms. DuBois, you can't contact anyone from here to let them know your plans. As a matter of fact, we will be supplying you with another mobile phone once you arrive in D.C. You can contact your family then. We need to get you out of here as soon as possible."

"Is there something that you are not telling me?"

"Ms. DuBois, please know that we only have your safety in mind. The less you know, the better off you are. You will be escorted back to your room and one of my men will be outside your door. He will then lead you to your escort team who will make certain you make your flight."

"What about some of the other people who work at the station? I was told that we were all leaving together tomorrow."

"You will be leaving alone. Everyone else will be taken care of."

For some reason after I left, I felt that I was not being told the entire story. But I figured I should follow their orders; despite the fact I badly wanted to call Sweezy to let him know what was going on. I knew that he and Chardonnay were probably worried out of their minds about me. Although I had survived some of the most horrific experiences in my life over the last few days, words could not explain how happy I was to know that Ty was alive.

Chapter 33

I was ready to kiss the ground when we landed at Reagan Airport. I was placed at the Willard and told that the First Gentleman, Ronald Isler, wanted to meet with me later that afternoon to talk about my work in the Middle East. It was overwhelming because I had not thought about any of the political implications when I was broadcasting in the Middle East. My concern was bringing to the forefront the plight of women who had been denied basic human rights for far too long. However, now I was going to meet the first African American Gentleman of the United States.

I was not politically inclined, and in fact, tried to remain far from it; but the U.S. had chosen its first transgendered female president. However, the media afforded more attention to the First African American Gentleman over the President because of his controversial civil rights involvement in Black and Brown Lives Matters 2. During the Trump Administration, the tension between law enforcement officers and people of color, particularly African Americans and Latinos, escalated to unprecedented levels. There was civil unrest in almost every city across America. The First Gentleman aggressively advocated for a civil revolution in order to enforce and protect the rights of black and brown people and won. There were major reforms in every major city when it came to the manner in which law enforcement dealt and interacted with underprivileged communities. Law enforcement officers had little interaction with these communities and with the assistance from grants provided by the federal government, many communities successfully policed themselves.

Regardless, I was excited about meeting the First Gentleman who insisted on me calling him Ron. Ron and his wife's election to the White House would forever change the landscape of American history. According to Ron, he loved the way that the "most powerful couple in the world was forcing America to address sexual identity, race and gender relations in ways that they could never have imagined eight years ago." Just having the opportunity to meet the First Gentleman seemed so surreal to me, because D.C. politics was a long way away from the realities of the hood where I grew up.

Ron personally gave me a tour of the White House that exceeded my expectations. I was amazed by the beauty and regal nature of the White House. But seeing President Obama and First Lady Michelle Obama's picture gracing the wall of the Grand Staircase gave me a feeling of being proud to have witnessed their eight year administration.

I expected that my visit would be a photo-opportunity for the First Gentleman. I would spend about ten minutes with him as the cameras clicked, he would thank me for what I had supposedly done for female rights in the Middle East. But there were no cameras, nor press. Instead, Ron and I had an intimate dinner where he shared a lot of his life with me, including how he had no idea that his wife was transgendered when they first met. He admitted to me that he had a difficult time accepting her; but after a while, he realized that love is love, no matter the race, creed, color, gender or identity.

He also revealed that the battle was more about how people would perceive him. He wanted to maintain his image as a heterosexual male. He eventually realized that he still was a heterosexual male who fell in love with a woman who was just as beautiful on the inside as she was on the outside.

It was beyond any story that I had ever heard, and I knew that one day their story would make it to the big screen. More than anything, I was surprised that this brother was so real; he reminded me a lot of Big John from back in the day. I left with the impression that he was making a lot of behind-the-scene decisions for the country, and it made me extremely proud that he was in the position to make a difference.

I was about to leave the White House when President Prescott-Isler made her appearance. The minute she entered the room, you could feel her energy and zest for life. I had never paid much attention to her; but she was stunning at forty-five-years old. If there was not so much coverage about her being a transgendered female, there was nothing about President Prescott-Isler that indicated that in a former life she was born a male. Ron introduced me to her and I extended my hand and she grabbed me as if I were her long-lost cousin.

"Porchia, I cut my meeting short with the Senate Finance Committee to meet you. Besides them being a bunch of boring politico humdrums, I just had to lay eyes on you. When Ron told me that you were visiting him today, I told him that there was no way I would miss meeting the woman who single-handedly changed the way that women are treated in the Middle East. We need you here to help us change our race relation issues that we are having here."

She caught me off guard and I was not sure how to respond. I gathered my thoughts and said, "Madam President, you are giving me way too much credit. There was a team of us dedicated to pursuing this effort. I just happened to be in the right place, at the right time."

"First of all, I am London. I detest that term, Madam President. No one ever used the term Sir President. Second, you are just being modest, I have followed your work. Third, I would love for you to think about how you can help America come to grip with the fact that white people are not the supreme rulers of this land."

I laughed out loudly and said, "Madam President."

Before I could finish my sentence, she waved her index finger like Mutombo, gave me a stern look, and shouted, "Ms. Porchia!"

"My bad, I mean London, I don't know if Jesus came down and walked the earth again to tell them that they were not that they would believe Him."

We all shared a good laugh before I left the White House. I hoped she clearly understood that I did not want anything to do with American politics. I had my share of trying to change things, while watching people die all around me.

The fact that I almost lost Ty was enough to keep me out of that arena for a while. My mind began processing what happened over the last couple of weeks, and I began feeling anxious. I was ready to see Ty because I still had some reservations about what they said to me. I know I could not completely see the charred and mangled body, but it looked like Ty that I saw at that morgue.

The driver asked if I wanted to see any of the other sights. I informed him that I had visited D.C. before and I was anxious to go back and relax at the hotel. Once I reached the hotel, I decided to go to get a drink at the bar just off the lobby. When I walked in, it seemed like the place was crawling with blue, gray, and black suits, which turned me off. So I decided to head to my room to order a drink.

As I was walking toward the elevator, I heard someone say loudly, "Oh, now that I have risen, you are going to ignore me."

I looked back and it was Ty. I ran to him and said, "Ty, is it really you? It is so good to see you!" I screamed while kissing and holding him tightly.

"Oh, if I knew that I would get this type of reaction, I would die more often."

"Ty, that is not funny! How are you?"

"How do I look?" he said stepping back and revealing his Alexander Amosu suit, which was easily distinguished by looking at the buttons.

"What the heck? I have been worried about you and you have been shopping!"

"No, I was trying to look good for you."

"Ty, you are a sight for sore eyes," I walked toward him again, and gave him a big embrace that he reciprocated with a kiss on my forehead. I then pulled back and said, "You would look good to me if you walked in wearing a rice sack. I thought I had lost you. I didn't know how I was going to face Penny."

"I talked with her and she told me to tell you hi, and that she sends her love."

"Oh my goodness, I still have not talked to Sweezy and Chardonnay. I need to call them. But I was hoping that I would know when we were going home because I know that is what they would want to know. Plus, I was promised a phone, and have not received one yet."

"Slow down Pocahontas, slow down. I would like to spend a little time with you here before we rush home."

"Rush? Ty, it has been quite an ordeal. We probably both need to be in a comfortable environment."

"But I think I would like to celebrate before we go home," said Ty.

"Celebrate!" I exclaimed. "You barely escaped death!"

"Yes, that is a reason to celebrate don't you think?" Ty asked.

"Yes, Ty. It is a reason to be thankful to God and right now I am so thankful to Him for all that He has done, and He continues to do."

Ty smiled and said, "Yes, I am thankful to Him and would be even more thankful to Him if you said yes."

"I don't know about staying, Ty. I am ready to go home."

"No, not about us staying," said Ty while getting on his knees. "You saying yes to marrying me." He fumbled with getting something from his pocket. He then pulled out a ring.

I stood there in shock, my tongue and lips were frozen.

Ty went on to say, "This ring survived me being kidnapped by the freedom fighters. When I told you that I was going shopping, I was going shopping for this ring. The freedom fighters actually took it from me, but they gave it back to me upon my release. They convinced me that I was the luckiest man on earth. And that Allah had his hands on me. I had a lot of conversation with the freedom fighters, so they knew my story. The leader, Jabbaar Ayoub, whose surname means messenger of Allah, told me that I would be released and that you would marry me. So what do you say Pocahontas. Was he right?"

I was shocked by Ty's reference to the terrorists as freedom fighters and what almost seem like an admiration of them; but so overcome by his story that tears just began flowing from my eyes. I then felt a warm presence embrace me.

Suddenly, a bright light emerged from behind Ty, and a voice spoke and said, "Remember your prayers and that I Am with you."

Then I heard Aunt Hattie say, "Baby girl, don't keep that man waiting any longer!"

I looked around and there was a couple standing watching us, the woman was nodding her head and mouthing, "Just say yes."

I pulled Ty's arms up so he could stand. Once he stood I looked into his eyes and saw love in its purest form. I knew because of The Presence, The Light, The Voices, The Affirmation, and The Love, I could not say anything other than, "Yes!"

Without uttering a single word, Ty gave me a long passionate kiss right in the middle of the lobby. The lady who nodded her head and mouthed yes to me shouted to people, "She said yes!"

Immediately I heard applause, but it did not stop our kiss. It reminded me of the first time he kissed me. My knees became wobbly, my heart raced, and I felt a wetness between my legs. My heart was clapping and doing a happy dance, but this time I was also saying,

"Thank you Lord, I have finally given myself permission to trust, love and to be loved. I am taking a chance on Ty, and asking for you to take the lead in our lives. Lord, I know that you have given me permission to love myself by allowing Ty to love me, and *if loving me is wrong, I don't want to be right.*